I0712803

FEATHER AND THE RIDDLE OF ANUBIS

A BOOK ABOUT LOVE, LOSS, AND EGYPTIAN MAGIC

CHRIS RAMEY

ILLUSTRATED BY SARA WILLIA

A beautiful tribute to the late Destry Ramey, who was a kind soul and a true friend to the animals.
—Catherine Ryan Hyde, author of *Pay it Forward* and 40 other novels

I was mesmerized from the get-go by this book. *Feather and the Riddle of Anubis* will transport readers into an ageless narrative search for answers. Ramey deftly guides the reader through a myriad of emotions as our star, Feather, follows her intuitions through a labyrinth of clues until she finds understanding, turning pain into beauty. It is a true heart-jerker and a loving tribute to a woman who was obviously very loveable.
—Dorothy Lehmkuhl, coauthor of *Organizing for the Creative Person*

Feather and the Riddle of Anubis is a beautiful love story between a chihuahua and the owner who rescued this sweet creature—or was it the other way around? It also honors the author's amazing mother, who inspired this story of adventure and love laced with a little bit of magic.
—Del Shores, writer, director, stand-up

Feather and the Riddle of Anubis is a treasure that will appeal to a range of readers from young children to adults, especially those with furry friends. The author has woven magic, humor, and education into a most delightful story inspired by the real Feather. Anyone with an imagination will be captured by this almost believable story and will enjoy the beautiful illustrations throughout.
—Linda Yates, founder and former director of Good Samaritan Children's Therapy Unit

This is a beautifully enlightened tale about finding peace, letting go, and honoring the spirit. I could not imagine a more fitting way to honor a woman I believe would indeed transcend the spiritual world to place peace upon the hearts of those she loved.
—Kathryn Michelle, codirector of the film *The Accursed*

Published by See What's Not Said Publishing, San Luis Obispo, California.

This is a work of fiction. Several characters, namely Feather, Feather's Mom, and Dr. Hawass, are based on real people, or a dog that thinks she is a person, though their perceptions and insights are used fictitiously. Additionally, incidents, conversations, and some places have been fictionalized.

Cover design and interior art by Sara Willia.
Exterior layout by Michelle Fairbanks.
Interior layout design by Qamber Designs.

LIBRARY OF CONGRESS
CATALOGING-IN-PUBLICATION DATA IS AVAILABLE

Hardcover ISBN: 979-8-9859138-0-4

1st Edition, March 30, 2022

For speaking engagements or to just connect with the author,
contact Chris at livefromsandiego@gmail.com

Printed in the United States of America

ABOUT THE AUTHOR

This book honors Destry Ramey's legacy. Chris was inspired by the deep bond between her and her rescue dog Feather, a curious, loving Chihuahua mix. When not writing, Chris runs an executive coaching company that specializes in Neuro-linguistic Programming and emotional intelligence. He and Feather divide their time between California's Central Coast and northern Mexico. As a former survival specialist with the US Navy and a cancer survivor, he is no stranger to difficulties. Chris believes in fiction's ability to bring insight into our personal challenges. He has lived internationally and visited over fifty-five countries, including Egypt, which was the last trip he took with his mother before her passing in 2020. This book is the fulfillment of a promise he made to her.

ABOUT THE ILLUSTRATOR

Sara Willia has worked as an illustrator for editorial pieces, children's literature, short stories, and YA fiction. Her editorial projects include illustration work for Accr and Acadiana Profile. Other work includes illustration for books written by Rick Cross (*Stories from the Godtable*), Kelley Usery Smith (Echo in the Veil series), and Tom Bristow (*Tex and the Long and Short of It*). Sara enjoys pretending to be a tree while she watches people from her top-story flat, shared with her beloved partner in Edinburgh, Scotland.

March 30th, 2020

It would be so easy to admire my mother just for her years of overcoming her health challenges. When many of us think of a survivor, a fighter, the name Destry Ramey immediately comes to mind. It's rare to hear of a person who has consistently battled and triumphed over a medical challenge, much less seven times in their lifetime, and yet that was my mom.

But my mother would be the first to ask me not to focus on health, disease, medical challenges, or any limiting factor. If we only focused on this one aspect of her life, it would be easy to miss what was so amazing, unique, and utterly incredible about her: her ability to touch the hearts of those around her.

Destry Ramey: mom, sister, aunt, godmother, pediatric nurse practitioner, flight attendant, children's author, animal lover, and one of the most kind, considerate, and loving friends many of us have ever known.

As her son, I am still trying to understand how a single person was able to be so many different things to so many people – but that was the magic and beauty of Destry Ramey.

Mom's optimism was legendary; her enthusiasm couldn't be contained. She was always looking for the positive in every situation, and her generosity and love were unmatched.

Mom had her own personal struggles and challenges like all of us, and yet you would almost never know it. Mom channeled her energy into helping others. When you needed somebody you could depend on or who had your back, she was always there.

My mother was also the most amazing adventurer that I have ever known. She always said "YES!" to traveling and any experience I suggested. Mom loved foreign cultures and people. Together, we were fortunate enough to visit fifty countries—from riding a merry-go-round in the rain in Paris to sneaking past a "do not enter" sign and crawling on our hands and knees down the lower antechamber of the Great Pyramid of Giza in Egypt.

Mom was always game for adventure, from swimming with sea turtles in tropical waters to hiking twelve miles in one day to visit the ancient city of Petra to scaling the upper rafter beams of a 500-year-old church in Quito, Ecuador, without railings or protection.

Mom's graciousness and kindness were international as well. People who didn't speak English or Spanish were still able to understand Mom because of the kindness and compassion she exuded.

One of the things I admired most about my mom was her ability to grow and reinvent herself. It is easy to accept things as they are, but Mom had a nonstop striving for understanding and self-betterment.

Mom adored Christmas so much she named her human child Chris. In addition, she also celebrated and decorated for every holiday. She loved bringing people together and used holidays as an excuse to share in the joy and happiness she felt in these moments.

Mom believed that whenever you saw a feather, it meant that your angel was nearby. Her little dog, Feather, the love of her life—her "favorite child" as I called her—gave Mom years of joy and happiness. So before Mom passed, we jokingly agreed that I would forever be known as the second favorite child. Not a day has passed since then that Feather hasn't reminded me of her preferred status.

On one of Mom's last physical days here in this world, I asked her to give me advice that would help me to navigate the world without her physical presence. Her advice was surprisingly simple. She said there are only two things that you need to remember:

1. Be as incredibly kind as you can to others.
2. Always seek balance in every aspect of your life.

My mother was truly a light who touched so many lives. The next time you find yourself in front of a candle, would you be kind enough to light it in honor of Destry Ramey? She will continue to spread her light way beyond her years on this earth.

Mom, Feather and I love you and miss your physical presence. I look forward to honoring and representing you for the remainder of my days here until you and I are able to be together again.

The day Mom met her favorite child.

TABLE OF CONTENTS

INTRODUCTION BY DR. ZAHI HAWASS

Jan. 1, 2022

Chris Ramey has written a charming story of the adventures of the adorable dog Feather, who learns many important lessons about love, loss, and Egyptian magic. Feather's travels through Egypt will inspire children to learn about the country in a fun and playful way. This story will capture many young minds and inspire a lifelong passion for ancient Egypt.

When I began working in archaeology, I did not think this would be my career, so I went back to my government job as an inspector of antiquities. One day, the head of the antiquities department asked me to be part of an excavation team in the desert region of the Delta. There, the workmen found a tomb and asked me to come and excavate it. In the middle of the tomb, I found a statue of Aphrodite, the Greek goddess of beauty. When I began to brush the statue, I realized I had found my love and passion.

I have had great adventures in my life but none so exciting as my latest excavation at Saqqara. There, I found a shaft about forty feet deep that led to a sealed door. When the workmen opened the door, we found ourselves in a room with a sealed limestone sarcophagus that is 4,200 years old. The lid weighed three tons, and the sarcophagus was seven tons. When we opened the lid about half a foot high, I put my head inside and found a big surprise: a beautiful female mummy and a crown made of leather and gold. Her body was wrapped entirely in bands of gold.

Artifacts like this will be displayed in the Grand Egyptian Museum, whose opening the whole world is waiting for. I began the construction of this museum in 2002 with the intention to open it in 2015, but trouble in Egypt in 2011 stopped my dream. We hope that on November 4th, 2022, the museum will open upon the 100-year anniversary of the discovery of the tomb of King Tutankhamun. I hope this book inspires a new generation to go out and find their passion, whatever it may be.

Dr. Zahi Hawass

FEATHER AND THE RIDDLE OF ANUBIS

A BOOK ABOUT LOVE, LOSS, AND EGYPTIAN MAGIC

CHRIS RAMEY

ILLUSTRATED BY SARA WILLIA

CHAPTER ONE

THE DREAM

What the mind needs, the dream reveals.—Ramses the XIII

Curled and cuddled in the midday sun, Feather and Egress slumbered in their afternoon siesta. Feather's new sister, Egress, a pug, heard Feather whimper and murmur a strange phrase: "A new beast, a new beast."

Asleep on her back, Feather's legs flitted in the air. She called out louder, almost crying, "A NEW beast, a NEW beast. Please explain to me. I don't understand!"

Egress stood up and gently touched Feather's tummy with her paw. "Wake up, Feather, wake up!"

Feather, slightly startled, looked around, yawned, and stretched her slender little legs.

"I'm confused, Egress," said Feather. "Was I dreaming?"

"You were talking and running in your sleep," Egress explained. "You kept repeating the words 'A new beast, a new beast.' What is a new beast?"

"I have no idea," Feather said. "All I remember is looking at myself in the mirror. Suddenly, a massive muscular dog wearing a jeweled gold collar stared right back at me. He looked like a larger version of me.

"He knew I was sad about losing Mom and that there was no time for me to rest; Mom needed me to know something! When I asked him what he meant, he unraveled an old brown scroll and made me promise to memorize the following words:

"Follow your heart, and it will guide you. Search in the Land of the Cobra, and when the city disappears, the place of dreams will illuminate your heart. Peace and understanding will then be forever yours."

"What on earth does that mean, Egress?"

"Feather, I don't have any clue," said Egress. "It sounds confusing, like a puzzle or maybe a riddle. Let me jot it down."

Together, they mulled over the riddle that Egress had written down.

"The dream makes me think of all the joyful and special times that I had with Mom. All the places that she took me, all the amazing adventures that we went on. I miss her so very much," Feather sniffled.

When Feather was first discovered, alone and abandoned in a brown paper bag on the side of the freeway, Egress and the other pugs raced to her rescue. They surrounded her, shielding her from enormous cars that whizzed within inches of smashing the bag that held her.

Later, Mom told her, "When I heard about this tiny baby puppy that someone had thrown away like garbage, I knew that you and I were destined to be together. I have always been a survivor, fighting cancer for so many years. Feather, you are just like me, an amazing soul that was destined to survive. Now we can support each other and appreciate every single day that we get to spend together!"

It had been nine months since Feather lost her mother. Even though some days held more laughter and joy, the sadness was still often unbearable.

Feather had also lost her sister Kippy a few years before. Even though she missed her sister's company and playful nature, there was nothing like losing a parent.

"I will never forget the moment when Mom first saw me," said Feather. "Mom raced over, scooped me up, and pulled me against her chest. Within seconds, our heartbeats were synchronized in a beautiful rhythm that was uniquely ours."

At that moment, she had understood what it felt like to be wanted and appreciated. Her mom never left her alone and insisted that Feather accompany her absolutely everywhere.

She taught Feather all the important lessons that moms do. She introduced her to dog lovers and even those who didn't love

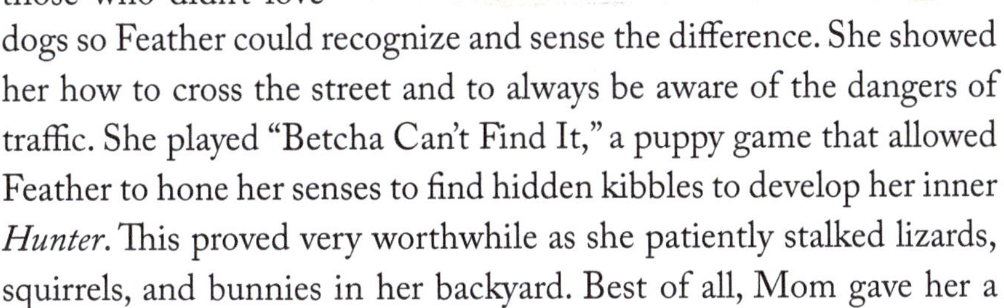

dogs so Feather could recognize and sense the difference. She showed her how to cross the street and to always be aware of the dangers of traffic. She played "Betcha Can't Find It," a puppy game that allowed Feather to hone her senses to find hidden kibbles to develop her inner *Hunter*. This proved very worthwhile as she patiently stalked lizards, squirrels, and bunnies in her backyard. Best of all, Mom gave her a

hearty meal twice a day, and taught her the importance of kitchen patrol—monitoring the floor for those food items that magically wound up there.

The thing that Feather missed most about her mom was their evening routine. Every night, they would slow down and cuddle together in a big, soft recliner. Mom loved to watch holiday movies, and Feather curled up under the blanket and snuggled tightly next to her. It was warm, safe, and surprisingly even better than food.

She loved hearing Mom tell the story about how Feather earned her name. "When I was a little girl, my grandmother, your Bonmama, used to tell me that whenever I saw a feather, it meant that an angel was nearby. So I decided to always keep my angel right nearby by naming you Feather. To me, you will always be my most special, littlest angel."

Her mom also taught her the meaning of the acronym ITALY, which stood for "I totally appreciate and love you." It was a special term just between them for whenever they had to say goodbye.

Feather returned to the present, her eyes clouded with tears and not so distant memories. "Egress, what happens to us after we die? Where do we go? Will I ever see Mom again?" she whispered.

"I really don't know, little one. I like to think that someday, when some time has passed, we will get to be with all those we have loved and lost," Egress said.

"But where? When? How?" Feather asked.

"I'm not really sure, Feather, but I truly believe that someday we will know."

"Someday is fine," said Feather, "but I have a riddle and a message from Mom that I need to unravel now!"

CHAPTER TWO

THE DOCTOR'S INVITATION

Sometimes the best way to understand yourself is to be lost in another world.—The Book of Them

Egress watched a program on YouTube through partially opened, oh-so-sleepy eyes as she and Feather lounged on the sofa. Feather lay on her back, daydreaming and pondering whether she would rather have a bowl of chewy or crunchy chicken strips.

Egress's head suddenly jolted up to full attention. A statue of a big, muscular black dog with a jeweled gold collar appeared before her on the screen. "Feather, Feather, look! Is that like the dog of your dream?"

Feather stared at the screen in disbelief. "Oh my gosh, Egress, that is him! Yes, that is him exactly."

Both dogs, now totally transfixed on the monitor in front of them, watched a man with an explorer hat talk about the dog of Feather's dream. The man introduced himself as Dr. Hawass, a famous archeologist and Egyptologist. He explained that this guardian of the afterlife's job, was to protect all those who have died. It was his job to hand deliver the souls of this world carefully into the next life, the afterlife.

"The Egyptians believe in a unique and special scale that this god of the afterlife uses to weigh every person against one single feather," Dr. Hawass said.

Feather loved that her name was also an important symbol in Egyptian mythology.

"If a person's heart was light and pure, then the feather would weigh more, and the guide would escort the person on their journey.

As the guardian, he would cross the bridge with the spirit of the deceased from our world and into the next. The guardian's name was Anubis," he said.

Both dogs' mouths dropped open at the same time. A new beast. A-nu-beast…A-nu-bis—Anubis!

"I wasn't talking about a new beast, Egress, I was saying the name of this guardian of the afterlife, Anubis! The dog who read me the scroll and said he had a message from Mom is named Anubis."

Feather looked at Egress. "How is this even possible? How could I have dreamt this, E? I have never ever seen or heard of Anubis before." Still in shock, she returned her attention to the program.

"Come see all the ancient wonders that Egypt has to offer," Dr. Hawass continued.

The video flew over an endless desert of sand. It reminded Feather of the warm evening walks on the beach with Mom as the cool water moistened and lapped at her small paws.

Unlike the beaches she knew here at home, she couldn't see any water in this video. Instead, there were three large triangular buildings, the pyramids of Egypt. Beside them stood a gigantic statue that looked like a dog lying down. Weirdly, it had the head of a person.

"Why on Earth did they put the head of a person on the body of an animal? That just doesn't make any sense!" Feather said.

"The Great Pyramid of Giza is the last remaining ancient wonder of the world," said Dr. Hawass. "Beside it sits one of the oldest and largest statues in the world, the mysterious Sphinx. It is believed to be the guardian of the pyramids and is represented by the face of a man with the body of a lion."

Feather's tail started wagging uncontrollably. The Sphinx wasn't a dog but a cat! She loved cats. She had spent countless days in her neighbor's backyard playing with her feline friends Basil, Tori, and Blue. Though she tried, she could never quite outmaneuver their quick reflexes.

The pyramids now faded from view, revealing massive buildings and statues carved out of an enormous mountain. "Abu Simbel is another breathtaking sight. Built by the great King Ramses II, this temple took over twenty years to sculpt."

Dr. Hawass guided them across another place he called Luxor to the Valley of the Kings, revealing underground burial tombs full of beautiful wall carvings and murals. "This is where archaeologists found the greatest discovery ever—King Tutankhamun's tomb," Dr. Hawass said.

Mom had told Feather all about the young King Tut. "He dealt with a disability his whole life and ended up being the most famous and well-known king of ancient Egypt," Mom had said. Feather admired anyone who overcame life's challenges.

Feather took it all in, just like her supper. What an amazing place! The valley disappeared behind a shiny new building made of steel and glass. Dr. Hawass stepped out in front of the building, beaming as though proud of the quick adventure he had just narrated.

"So you are probably wondering, 'Where should I begin?' Well, that's an easy one," he said. "Come join me at the brand new Grand Egyptian Museum. "Here you will see the most famous piece of Egyptian art ever found, the mask of King Tutankhamun. Egypt is magical, mysterious, and mystical. Here you can find solutions and solace to your greatest needs. So come, follow your heart, and it will guide you…Here in the Land of the Cobra, you will discover the secrets to eternal life from the clues that the ancients left us thousands of years ago."

Feather sat up. "Wait a minute, did he just say the first part of the message from the scroll?" She glanced at what Egress had written down earlier.

Feather read aloud, "Follow your heart, and it will guide you. Search in the Land of the Cobra, and when the city disappears, the place of dreams will illuminate your heart. Peace and understanding will then be forever yours."

"That's it," squealed Feather. "I need to follow my heart to Egypt. Egypt is the Land of the Cobra."

Feather paced the room, going back and forth as if she were stalking an invisible adversary. She burst out, almost shrieking, "I know what I need to do. I must go to Egypt to find the answers to eternal life. Oh, Egress, do you think I will understand what Anubis told me about Mom there?"

That evening ended up being a very long and sleepless night for Feather.

CHAPTER THREE
FRIENDS, FEARS, FACTS, AND FICTION

What we fear most, is what we don't yet understand.—Sara of Scotland

The next morning, Feather raced over to her neighbor's and best friends, Basil, Tori, and Blue.

She burst into their yard and exclaimed in one breath, "Guess what? Tomorrow I'm flying to Egypt 'cause I'm on a quest for the afterlife, and I need to figure out the secret riddle that Anubis gave me so I can understand my mom's message, and the only person who can help me figure this all out is Dr. Hawass, the greatest living Egyptologist!" She plopped down onto her belly, completely winded.

When Feather caught her breath, she looked up to find her favorite felines staring at her. Each one had been preoccupied with themselves until Feather raced into their yard.

Basil was in the middle of a private grooming moment. He adjusted his legs to look more presentable for their guest.

Tori, counting clouds on a bed of catnip, lay on her back, head tilted, cross-eyed. She moved her gaze to Feather for three full seconds and then calmly returned to her patch of catnip, quietly mumbling, "The afterlife has always been my friend!"

Puzzled, Blue swept tenderly up to Feather. "Feather, I really want to understand what you're talking about." He gently nudged his head against Feather's fur. "But I need you to slow down, please. Okay?"

Feather nodded, the tip of her nose warming quickly with a tinge of embarrassment.

"So," said Blue, giving Feather fur-to-fur contact, "slowly and concisely, okay, Monkey Rat?"

This nickname, Monkey Rat, instantly made Feather smile.

Years ago, Basil remarked how Feather darted around and could balance things in her paws, just like an animated little monkey. "You're as clever as a rat and can get yourself out of the stickiest of situations," he'd said. So the name stuck with her very best friends.

Feather lifted herself back up to all four paws again. "Sorry, guys, I'm just so nervous and excited!"

She slowed down as she described her dream, discovering Anubis, his riddle, and watching Dr. Hawass. She finished her tale by mentioning that her mom had a message to give her.

The cats sat back, deep in contemplation.

Tori finally broke the silence and said, "Well, I personally have always loved Egypt, even as a little kitten."

"That has nothing to do with the fact that cats were worshiped as gods there, does it?" Basil asked.

"Of course not!" And then, after a very long, telling pause, Tori admitted, "Well, maybe. Okay, yeah, that is honestly the coolest thing I have ever heard in all of my lives. I mean, can you imagine? 'Human, go fetch me a large boneless chicken breast, and then you can hand-feed me at my private catnip garden overlooking the Nile.'"

"Feather," Blue said, "why are you shivering? Do I detect some fear in your voice?"

"I'm terrified," Feather replied. "I hate to admit it, but I'm really scared."

Almost in unison, all three cats gave their own supportive encouragement.

"Talk to us, Feather," said Basil.

"It's all going to be chill, Monkey Rat," Tori said.

"How can we put your mind at ease?" asked Blue, tenderly grooming Feather with his whiskers.

"I think the mistake I made was looking on the internet this morning to learn more about Egypt. I just wanted to be prepared," Feather said. "But I read that Egypt is crowded and dangerous, especially the traffic.

"I also read that the locals seem to be wary of people or animals who are not Egyptian." Feather trembled. "And then it just hit me—I'm not Egyptian! I am a mix of Mexican Chihuahua, Polish Pomeranian, and just a little bit of Chinese Pug. And then there is this whole fear of death, and what exactly is the afterlife?"

Blue glanced knowingly at Basil and ever so gently embraced Feather's tail in his.

"Feather," asked Basil, "are you scared because you've never left home or been alone before?"

Feather had never realized this before. Speechless, she started chewing on her left paw.

"Listen, Monkey Rat. You can't believe everything you read on the internet," drawled Tori. "I read once that someone thought too much catnip was bad. I mean seriously, bro, can you imagine? Talk about the unenlightened!"

"Feather, I want to share some helpful advice," said Blue. "When something is foreign or we don't really understand it, it's easy for us to label it as bad."

Feather nodded, a little confused.

"Many times, we need to sort things out in our minds as either good or bad," Blue mused. "When we are not familiar with something, we can't put it in our good pile because we don't have any experience with it yet. So it is easier for us to put it in the bad pile. Does that make sense? Think of it like a package at the post office."

"It does actually, thank you." Feather nodded. "So the key is being open to new discoveries and possibilities even though it would be easier to be afraid of change or something new?"

"That's it Feather! I notice you aren't shivering anymore," Blue said. "Remember that fear is nothing more than curiosity that has yet to be explained."

"Now, as far as understanding death and the afterlife, it all comes down to the serenity of a litter box," said Basil.

"A litter box? You know I don't use those. What do you mean?" asked Feather.

"I think what he means is that the three of us might not always agree with each other's beliefs," Tori began, looking at the other cats, "but if we can share the same litter box, then we most certainly can be open to the possibility of different ideas about what happens to us when we die."

"Well, I suppose that makes sense," said Feather.

Feather shuddered at the thought of death. All it conjured was the absence of her beloved mother and sister. It was not an easy concept to understand, but she would try. Right now, she felt alive;

Figuring out if some

anything beyond that was hard to comprehend. Still, she reminded herself of Blue's wisdom.

"Why doesn't everyone believe the same thing?" Feather asked.

Basil jumped in. "I don't know if you know this, Feather, but the three of us came from very different homes. Each of our owners believed in different things," he said.

"For example, my first owners were called Christians. They believed that when we die, we go to a place called Heaven," Blue began. "They said that we would meet again with all our relatives who had passed and that there would always be fresh milk and honey." He looked at Feather. "Oh, I'm sorry for mentioning food, Monkey Rat."

"I know. At just the mere mention of food—*bam*—like a floodgate, the drool just comes forth," said Feather.

Tori reached into her bag of animal edibles and lobbed Feather a treat.

"What about you, Tori?" Feather asked.

"My family was, like, totally Zen, little dude," she said, swaying to some music that apparently only she could hear. "I mean, they

thing is good or bad.

were Buddhists, so they were all about achieving something called Nirvana. That's like the ultimate happiness. It's like searching and searching until you finally hit the catnip motherlode. Sure, they may die, but they will be reborn in order to use the lessons they learned in their previous lives."

"Isn't that like Hindus?" Basil asked Tori. "They believe in rebirth too, right?"

"A little," admitted Tori, "but if you were not good in the previous life, then you just might return as a jellyfish or a flea."

Gopher holes, the thought of fleas made Feather scratch and then chew again on her left paw.

"Another belief about the afterlife comes from Muslims. Now, they believe in a place called Jannah," Tori stated. "To them, it is a place of everlasting bliss where there is no pain, sickness, or sadness. In order to get to Jannah, you must have done more good than bad while here on Earth."

"Or there are some people, like in my first home, who didn't believe in any afterlife at all," Basil mentioned.

"But if you don't believe in an afterlife, what happens after you die?" asked Feather.

"To these individuals, the focus isn't on death but on life. It is about making the most of your time on earth," Basil said, twitching his whiskers.

"Jewish people have a slightly similar belief," said Blue. "They believe that any person, no matter their religion, who lives a loving and moral life here on Earth is invited to go to Heaven. They also believe our loved ones can not only see us from Heaven but also our good deeds and acts here on Earth that honor them will enhance their experience in the afterlife."

Feather was fascinated by all the incredible possibilities and beliefs. She sat back and listened intently as her friends discussed even more cultures, religions, and their unique beliefs. She imagined herself dressed in each cultures unique outfit.

When they were finished, she gave each of her friends an enormous hug and confirmed they would be at her departure tomorrow.

"We wouldn't miss it for the world," Blue said.

That night, Feather could hardly contain her excitement. Still, she knew she needed sleep for her adventure tomorrow. With a calm and yet curious mind, she had one of her best nights of sleep ever. Miraculously, she'd forgotten her fears, and unknowns now felt like opportunities.

CHAPTER FOUR
FEATHER'S FIRST FLIGHT

Often, the journey of our lifetime begins within ourselves.
—The Book of Destry

At almost exactly 5:45 a.m., a slow fog of fear and panic crept back into Feather's mind. She was so certain after speaking with Blue and the cats that she had eliminated all of her fear. Although Feather wasn't completely sure what her change of emotion meant, she did know that sometimes, like the weather, our moods can shift as well. She was just honoring her inner weather pattern.

So Feather decided she would not go to Egypt. Period. She grabbed her covers and buried herself right in the middle of them. Her plan was set.

Then Egress knocked on the door. In a little squeaking voice, Feather said, "No one is home, please come back tomorrow."

Egress put on her most energetic and cheery voice. "Somebody brought you a gift!"

That was all it took for Feather to emerge from her dark covers like a mini hurricane. She flew out the door, squealing, "Really, a gift for me?"

Egress held out a wrapped package. "Following in the tradition of your mom, one world-loving traveler, may this help you ascend to incredible new heights."

Feather tore open the box and found inside a 1940s green khaki aviator suit with bomber jacket, cap included.

She enveloped Egress in an enormous hug. "It's perfect. I love it, and I love you. Thank you, Egress."

Feather's flight was only hours away and she felt a sudden rush to get ready. Her new sister always knew how to encourage and motivate her.

Thirty minutes later, Feather emerged.

"Aren't you the cutest, most adorable mini aviator ever?" Egress looked away quickly to hold back a tear. "We should get a move on."

At the airport, Feather's early morning reluctance, now felt like a blur as she imagined her grand adventure. She stopped daydreaming momentarily to hear the announcement.

"Flight DR-1158 direct to Cairo, Egypt, will begin boarding at this time," announced the overhead speaker.

Feather's body buzzed with anticipation.

The loudspeaker echoed again. This time, the words sounded urgent. "We will begin by boarding any passengers needing extra assistance or anyone who is under two feet in height."

"That's you, Feather," Egress urged.

"But our friends haven't arrived to see me off," Feather said, casting around for them.

"I'm sure they meant to be here." Egress kissed her sister on the cheek.

"I love you, Egress," Feather sobbed and gave Egress the tightest hug possible.

"I love you, too, Feather, and can hardly wait to hear about all your adventures. Please be smart and careful," Egress said.

As Feather climbed the metal steps that would lead her to her very first plane ride, a mixture of excitement and nerves ran from the tip of her nose to the tip of her tail. She was actually doing it! She was heading on her quest for the afterlife.

She looked back over her shoulder but was swept up in hundreds of feet passing her by. *No friends came to see me off,* she thought sadly.

Once on board, she settled into her seat, brushed back a tear, and closed her eyes. Moments later, she opened her eyes to the pressure of someone gently touching her shoulder and one of the sweetest Southern accents she had ever heard. "Hi there, I'm Linda, your flight attendant. I just wanted to check in to see if you're okay, hon?"

"I'm okay," whimpered Feather.

"Are you sure, hon?" Linda asked.

It didn't take long before Feather told Linda about how she missed her friends and this was her first time doing anything alone.

Linda suddenly shifted her gaze past Feather and out the window, smiling and exclaiming, "Well, my goodness, you just never know what you are going to see here at the airport!"

Feather turned to look. There on the tarmac, behind a protective fence stood Feather's friends holding an enormous banner that read, "Who knew Monkey Rats could fly? Egypt will love you!"

She couldn't hear her friends, but they jumped up and down, shouting in her direction and waving.

Her tears suddenly dried up, and the slyest littlest smile sneaked across her mouth.

Suddenly, the engines rumbled beneath her. The airplane zoomed down the tarmac and leapt into the air as the airport disappeared from view.

She gasped at the jump of the plane hitting the air, but seeing all her friends cheering her on brought her peace of mind. She inhaled calmly, relaxed, and decided it was the perfect time for a catnap.

Later, Feather woke, startled to find her seat belt being forcibly pulled down around her. She struggled to loosen it, but it wouldn't budge. She looked out the window and saw… nothing. There was no land below. She heard the pilot on the intercom. "Umm, hey folks, we're cruising at thirty-five thousand feet and have been doing our best to avoid some larger turbulence. So just sit back, try and relax, and we should be out of it in the next five minutes or so."

Turbulence? Feather had no idea what that was. And then suddenly the plane dropped, almost as if all power had been lost. *This is not good*, she thought, chewing on her left paw. *No, not good at all.*

After what seemed like hours of agitation, where her stomach lifted up to the ceiling and then plummeted to the floor again, Feather plopped back against her seat when the turbulence calmed. She breathed a sigh of relief. All of sudden—*BOOM*—the plane bounced and rattled as if falling apart. Feather dug her claws into the seat, holding on for dear life. With her eyes closed, praying for safety, she again felt a soft touch on her shoulder.

She opened her eyes, and there looking down on her, was...her mom! Dressed in her old flight attendant uniform and smiling the most serene and loving smile possible, Mom lowered herself and whispered, "You've got this, my Littlest Angel, just breathe. I am always here watching over you!"

Feather gazed lovingly into her hazel eyes, felt the warmth of her presence, and scented the subtle fragrance that was uniquely Mom's. Was this another dream? Was she sleeping?

Feather closed her eyes, took three deep breaths, and reopened them.

Linda now stood where her mom had just been standing. Feather had to do a double take to make sure it wasn't Mom. "Miss Feather, time to wake up." Linda's voice nudged her gently from her slumber. "We will be landing in the next ten minutes."

Disoriented, Feather looked for her mother. With a sinking sensation, she realized that Mom was gone and would never come back. As the reality sunk in, she gazed without seeing into the darkness outside. She was certain she had just closed her eyes.

"It looks like someone was tired from all of the excitement!" Linda smiled and then handed Feather a piece of paper. "In order to gain entry into Egypt, you will need to give this form and your passport to the counter person at customs."

Feather grabbed her passport from her backpack and wrote down all the requested information on the form. She smiled, hardly able to believe that she was about to enter a different country and start her journey to understand the riddle from Anubis. She only wished that she was entering Egypt with her mother at her side. She completed the form and slid her passport back into the side pocket of her backpack.

Her head clearer now, Feather looked out into the dark, hoping she could see one of the three pyramids. She could only make out what looked like a stacked triangle. *I always assumed it would be larger.*

Once off the plane, Feather had never seen so many people—or lines—in all her life. She was also impressed by the incredible diversity. Every type of person, dog, cat, and quite a few goats, chickens, and sheep were waiting in lines as well. As she stepped into the line for customs, her eyes followed the meandering path all the way to the front. There had to be at least fifty or more people in front of her. *Yikes.* She would be here until midnight.

While she waited in line, a man literally covered in hats

approached her.

"Young lady, your aviator's cap is great," he bellowed from behind a flowery sun hat, "but now that you are here in Egypt, you are going to need some serious protection from our magnificent sun."

She caught sight of a beige explorer's hat and asked to try it on. The man handed her a mirror so that she could see. She looked… strangely familiar. From behind the mirror, the man said, "Now, that one is perfect. You look just like a little Dr. Hawass."

I knew I had seen this hat somewhere, she thought, remembering the video. She thanked and paid the man and returned her attention to the line. Incredibly, there were only a few people ahead of her now. Within seconds, she heard "Next passenger, please," and she stepped forward.

The customs agent smiled very briefly and sternly stated, "Passport and customs paperwork, please."

She grabbed her customs form and reached for her passport, but it wasn't there. She started rummaging through her backpack. Not there, not there, and not there! Her eyes clouded with tears. "I must have lost it somehow between here and the plane," she whimpered.

With a frown, he handed her a written sheet with thirteen steps to follow. "Sorry, we are closing in thirty minutes."

Feather plopped down into a little ball, frustrated and defeated, and started madly chewing on the rim of the hat that she had just bought. *What do I do?* she thought. *I can't contact anyone. Nobody knows me here.* She would have to sleep in the airport! *Wasn't Egress just hugging me? Why did I ever think I could do this trip on my own?*

"Feather, Feather," came a voice in the crowd. She knew that voice. It was Linda, the flight attendant, running toward her. "Feather, I have your passport, I found it under your seat!"

Feather ran toward her, eyes filling with tears of joy and relief.

"Oh, Linda, thank you so much—I had no idea what I was going to do," she admitted.

"Well, dontcha reckon we should get your adventure back on

track?" said Linda, bringing Feather to the front of the line. She said a few pointed words in Arabic to the customs agent in her Southern drawl. A few moments later, she waved goodbye to the taxi as Feather vanished into the Cairo night.

TAXI
7042013

CHAPTER FIVE
THE GRAND EGYPTIAN MUSEUM

A cat by any other name may not be a cat.—Willie De Coy

Feather awoke in unfamiliar surroundings. *This isn't my bedroom, these are not my sheets, and this most certainly isn't my bed,* she thought. She rubbed and removed the sleep dust from the corners of her eyes and coaxed herself to wake up. She felt tired, groggy, and unrested as if she hadn't slept at all—what a strange feeling. This room was darker than she was accustomed to. *Where am I?*

Feather sauntered from bed, threw open the dark curtains, and fell backward in awe, landing smack on her little butt. There stood the largest structure Feather had ever seen—the Great Pyramid of Giza—and it was absolutely stunning! *Egypt, I am in Egypt. Now I remember.*

Now, an internal brewing boiled under her skin and below her muscles. She was a little furry teapot about to spout off, and nothing was safe from her quest for curiosity. Like all good explorers, she was hopeful for the possibilities. "First, I will scarf down some morning kibbles, and then I'll head to the brand new Grand Egyptian Museum," she said aloud.

Feather made her bed, brushed her teeth, and washed her face, all the while unable to look away from the pyramid. She grabbed her Egyptian excavation hat, ran out of the hotel, and jumped into an awaiting taxi.

"The Grand Egyptian Museum, please," she told her driver. "How far is it from here?"

"Good morning," her driver said. "It is only 5.4 kilometers from here, about 3.5 miles approximately. We should arrive there in about one and a half hours."

"One and a half hours? So long?"

"Yes, there is quite a bit of traffic this time of morning," he said.

Feather gently chewed on her hat, but within minutes, she had completely forgotten about the time as the world outside bustled with activity that drew her attention. People were all in a hurry to be going someplace as though on a mission.

She saw so many different things: children heading to school and vendors selling newspapers, fresh vegetables, and fruits in beautiful outdoor markets. Hundreds of cars and even more scooters bustled past. A man even rode by on a moped carrying a goat on his shoulders. Talk about living in luxury! In the United States, goats usually had to carry things; here, the people carried the goats. She decided that if the Buddhists were right, she definitely wanted to come back as an Egyptian goat.

They arrived at the Grand Egyptian Museum about thirty minutes later. Puzzled, she looked at the driver, who simply smiled and winked, saying, "Traffic was kind to us today. I guess the ancients wanted to meet you early. Welcome, and enjoy yourself!"

Feather beamed.

As she exited the taxi, she instantly recognized the metal and glass building from the video with Dr. Hawass. She knew the museum would be impressive, but she was even more in awe at the theme of inverted triangles and pyramids all over the facade of the building.

As she proceeded through the main entry, she encountered an enormous statue with an inscription that read, *This famous 3000-year-old statue of Ramses II, weighing more than 83 tons, is now the first to welcome you to the new Grand Egyptian Museum, or GEM as it is affectionately known.*

She closed her eyes, touched the statue, and pretended she could see all the things that it had witnessed over its three millennia in Egypt.

Even though the museum was enormous—the largest archeological museum in the world, in fact—Feather knew exactly where she needed to go; she had first heard the message from

Dr. Hawass about the new King Tutankhamun exhibit. She labored up a massive staircase where she passed eighty-seven different statues of pharaohs and Egyptian gods.

At the top of the stairs, she turned to the right, went down a pathway, and entered the official King Tutankhamun area. A golden plaque with blue topaz read, *In front of you lies 75,000 square feet, holding more objects from King Tutankhamun's tomb than have ever been on display before.* Her little body tingled with anticipation. Everywhere she looked, she saw gold, gold, and more gold. Gold embedded with blue lapis lazuli, green turquoise, black obsidian, and bright red carnelian. She made a beeline past what felt like hundreds of jeweled gold relics, and made her way to King Tut's burial mask.

She entered a large darkened room and found herself eye to eye with the mask of King Tutankhamun. Her fur took on a golden glow as the mask's reflection pierced her with its luminescence. She eyed it up and down, looking for anything that might give her a clue about the message from Anubis.

The first things to catch her eye were the vulture and the cobra on the top of the mask. The riddle stated, "Come to the Land of the Cobra," and that land was Egypt. What about the vulture? What was the significance? She further inspected the mask, which had both ears pierced and a tremendous number of hieroglyphics written on the back.

Is the back of the mask the clue? Will I need to learn to read hieroglyphics? she wondered. She returned to the front and stared deeply into the eyes of the mask; suddenly she thought she saw movement. Wait, that couldn't be. She blinked her eyes a couple times and looked again. There was distinct movement again, a reflection around the blacks of the eyes. Transfixed, without blinking, the eyes looked almost catlike. At that exact moment, a solitary black hair gently descended from above and landed on Tutankhamun's nose.

She slowly gazed upward toward the ceiling. There, about fifteen feet above on a metal rafter, sat a long, thin black cat. It looked down at Feather, winked, smiled, and made a high-pitched trilling sound.

Within seconds, the cat took off, running along the thin metal beams above. Feather
watched the cat closely and followed fifteen
feet below. The cat leapt from beam to beam,
and Feather followed. Then, with another leap, the cat launched off
the beams and raced along the ground. *Holy kitty is she fast!* Feather
watched the long cat jump up in the air, spin around, and do a full
360-degree twist in the air, completely evading her. Feather was blown
away at the speed and flexibility of this cat. She had never seen these
kinds of acrobatics from any of her friends before. Three minutes, five
minutes, ten minutes later, Feather tried but just couldn't keep up, and
the cat disappeared.

Exhausted and frustrated from pursuing this quick-footed
feline, Feather gnawed on the rim of her hat. *Wait*, she thought, *I am*

not here to chase an Egyptian cat but to find the clues to the riddle from Anubis. So she sat up straight, removed her hat from her mouth, and spoke aloud the clues that she understood so far.

"Okay, so I saw the cobra on the mask of King Tut, so Egypt is indeed the Land of the Cobra, but I already knew that. I need something more."

A high-pitched, airy voice interrupted, "Egypt isn't the Land of the Cobra. Well, not exactly."

Feather looked up and found the strange cat in the corner directly across from her.

"What did you say?" asked Feather.

"Why were you chasing me?" asked the cat.

"I was excited to see you," Feather said. "I have never seen a cat like you before, and I love cats."

The cat made a hysterical high-pitched laugh. "I'm not a cat, you little Anpu, I am a weasel. I am a noble Egyptian weasel, to be exact."

Feather had been called many things in her life but never an Anpu.

"Anpu?" she asked.

The weasel paused for a moment and then cocked its head almost 180 degrees. "It basically means 'my new little friend.'"

"Oh, okay, thank you," said Feather, appreciative of the lesson and the kindness. "I have heard of weasels but have never seen one in person before. So is that why you are so long and fast?"

"Exactly." The weasel smiled. "It is my job to keep the museum free of rodents. And as you saw, I have the ability to get in and out of the tightest spots."

"Okay," said Feather, "but I am confused. You said that the cobra on King Tut's mask isn't the symbol for Egypt?"

"That is correct," said the weasel. "It isn't the symbol for all of Egypt; it is only the symbol for Lower Egypt. Just like the vulture next to the cobra is the symbol for all of Upper Egypt."

"That's it!" exclaimed Feather. "That is my clue. I know exactly where I need to go now. Thank you and take care, weasel. Sorry, I need to go to Lower Egypt," she said, flying toward the museum exit.

"But waaaaaaaaaaaaait," shouted the weasel, "I need to explain something to you!"

But Feather, on a mission and one step closer to understanding the riddle, was already gone.

CHAPTER SIX

THE GREAT PYRAMID OF GIZA

That which we most seek often hides in plain sight.
—The philosopher, Sirhc Yemar

Back at the hotel lobby, Feather dashed toward the concierge desk, realizing a little too late that she was running way too fast across the brass and marble floor. She skidded out of control and crashed into the desk, which spewed a volcanic explosion of papers into the air.

"Oh my gosh, oh my goodness, oh my heavens," said the concierge, dropping to his feet and helping the little ball of fur up onto the chair, "is the little Anpu hurt?"

"Just my pride, sir, just my pride. And thank you for calling me Anpu." Feather blushed hearing the same nickname in one day.

Embarrassed but excited, she said, "Sir, I must travel south to the places that Dr. Hawass mentioned in his video. Can you help me?" Surely this was where she would uncover the remaining clues to the riddle.

Mohammed, the concierge, explained that he had lived in Giza for the past sixty-seven years and would be more than happy to direct her. "The best way to visit these sites that you mentioned is to take a Nile River cruise. You will visit the Valley of the Kings in Luxor, a Nubian village near Aswan, and then continue on down to visit Abu Simbel, south of Lake Nassar."

Having never been on a boat before, Feather felt like such an adventurer and could hardly wait to fly out of Cairo and embark tomorrow morning from Luxor.

"Since your flight won't be leaving until 6:00 a.m. tomorrow, you still have plenty of time to see the pyramids and the Sphinx here in Giza. However, since traffic is sure to be congested right now, you should walk there. It will only take you about ten minutes or so."

"What a great idea," said Feather.

"Be sure to bring a large bottle of water," offered Mohammed. "It is super hot outside, and even though we are in the middle of the city, it is technically a desert."

"Can you please give me directions?" she asked.

"All you need to do is make a left out of the hotel and follow the majestic structure directly to the entrance."

Feather thanked him for his help, grabbed a tall bottle of water, and made her way toward the pyramid.

I have always loved a good walk, Feather thought, but here, walking to this ancient structure, she never could have imagined she would be visiting Egypt in her lifetime. Some of the oldest buildings in the United States were a couple hundred years old, but here, things were thousands of years old.

As she walked, Feather became aware of dozens of pairs of eyes on her. People were staring! She wasn't sure why. People and animals came from all over the world to visit Egypt, so why would they care about her?

When she reached the entrance to the pyramids after eight minutes of walking, she tapped the entrance guard on his shin. "I have a strange question for you. Do you know why people seem to be staring at me?"

He smiled kindly and said, "We love tourists and people from other cultures and countries. We are always so happy to share our customs and our history. We carefully watch to make sure that if anyone needs anything, we can instantly help. Plus, most of us have never seen a little tiny Anpu like you before." He winked.

Feather smiled at her new nickname. "Thank you, I appreciate that! You, too, are my new friend," she said.

Feather took a moment to ponder all the amazing nicknames that she had been given in her eight human years (fifty-six dog years) so far. Her favorite by far was her mom's nickname for her: Littlest Angel. She also loved being called Monkey Rat by her closest friends. Her new daddy, Chris, called her Mooky-Lau, although she wasn't really sure why. There was even that neighbor from Mexico who called her Chihuahuina, which meant "adorable chihuahua mixture." And now, here in Egypt, she earned her latest one: little friend, or Anpu.

As Feather walked toward the largest pyramid of the three, she thought about her assumption that the pyramids would be in the middle of the desert with no civilization nearby. But there were billboards and buildings and traffic and even some American fast-food restaurants. All of them were just right across the street. Suburban Cairo seemed to have crept out of the city and right up to the steps of these ancient wonders.

Feather made her way toward the Great Pyramid of Giza. The limestone blocks were enormous, as though built right up to the sky. *I am amazed that anyone could not only have made these enormous blocks but also stacked them as well,* she thought. She had read that there was still a lot of debate about when this pyramid was built, who exactly built it, how it was aligned so perfectly with the constellations, and, of course, why these three pyramids were not four sided but eight. The only way to see all eight sides was from a plane.

Feather chewed absent-mindedly on her hat as she took in this great pyramid, framed by the industry and activity from the city on all sides of it. Desert or not, this was a very active and busy part of Cairo, and the Great Pyramid surely had witnessed a lot of construction over the years.

Suddenly, panting heavily, her upper gums sticking to her canines, Feather started shaking, overwhelmed with heat. She hadn't drunk any water for a while. Not wanting to become dehydrated, or worse, get heat stroke, she reached for her water bottle in her backpack. Slick with condensation, it slipped right through her paws, hit the stony ground below and cracked open, spilling most of its contents.

"Flying fleas," she said, "now I need to find a garbage can and another bottle of water." She squatted down to carefully drink the remaining water in the broken bottle that hadn't yet seeped into the rocks and sand below.

Then she sat back up slowly and looked around dumbfounded. *What on Earth? Where did it go?* The three different pyramids and the Sphinx still stood before her, but the entire metropolitan city had vanished. Now only desert stretched out next to the four landmarks. How was this possible? She stepped a foot to the left and suddenly the hustle and bustle of the city returned. She moved to her right, and again it was gone.

At this specific spot and at this perfect height and angle, she seemed alone with the desert, the pyramids, and the Sphinx. The surrounding city was gone like it might have been thousands of years ago.

Suddenly smiling, she reached into her backpack and pulled out the riddle Egress had written down.

Follow your heart, and it will guide you. Search in the Land of the Cobra, and when the city disappears, the place of dreams will illuminate your heart. Peace and understanding will then be forever yours.

Excited and still surprised about the city disappearing, Feather said the next line of the riddle, "The place of dreams will illuminate your heart." The place of dreams. What exactly did that mean?

The city must have disappeared because there was something more here to discover. She tiptoed closer and closer to the pyramid until she could practically touch it and meticulously examined the limestone blocks, looking for something, anything. Alas, nothing jumped out at her.

Feather rummaged through her backpack and pulled out a magnifying glass, looking for hieroglyphics, but there weren't any. She looked for drawings but only saw a faint drawing of...a vase? Maybe that was the next clue. Maybe the vase was the place of her dreams? But she didn't remember a vase in her dreams. As she walked close up to the pyramid, the other two pyramids disappeared as well. The city was still gone, but the Sphinx was there in full view. The Sphinx had been in her dream with Anubis. *That must be it! When the city disappears, the place of dreams will illuminate my heart. The clue must be the Sphinx.*

She stepped away from the pyramid toward the direction of the Sphinx and felt… she wasn't sure what. Her heart fluttered; her breath moved fast and quick. Her heart must indeed be illuminated. This was it. She was about to solve the riddle and find out exactly what her mom wanted to tell her!

But wait a minute, she thought. *I still have to head south to Lower Egypt, toward the Land of the Cobra. The riddle can't possibly end here. That wouldn't make sense. Okay, so maybe my heart isn't quite illuminated yet,* she thought, *but there must be a reason for the city to disappear and point me in this direction.*

She grabbed the rim of her hat and chomped on it as she sprinted toward the Great Sphinx.

CHAPTER SEVEN

Sometimes a lifetime of understanding is only a few steps away.
—Jordan the Enlightened

Feather was still reeling from the city disappearing. How could that point her in the direction of the Sphinx when she still had to go to Lower Egypt?

She started at the front of the magnificent Sphinx next to the right front paw. The head sported the same type of headpiece that she had seen on King Tut's mask, and the face was definitely human.

"Okay, so what we have here," said Feather, speaking in her best television detective voice, "are unusually oversized paws. One might suppose," she continued, "that maybe this is not the original carving." *Could there have been something here before, and it eroded over time?*

"Maybe," she continued, "this was previously a statue of some-thing else—a person or a full-sized animal." Then her mind wan-dered, and her internal voice gently said, *Or maybe even Anubis?* The thought surprised her.

It was, after all, Anubis who had come to her in her dream, and the clue in the riddle spoke about the place of dreams. Maybe the Sphinx was actually the place of dreams, the place that Anubis had once guarded, the place where people passed from our Earth into the afterlife.

Satisfied with her investigation, she headed toward the body of the Sphinx. Surprisingly, there were not many tourists around it, just a couple of men near the base on the side of the monument.

She walked over to the men, who were dressed in light brown tunics, their faces and heads completely covered in makeshift masks

made out of old brown shirts. She could only see the silhouette of their heads and their eyes. One of them stopped working and walked over to her. He greeted her in perfect, yet heavily-accented English. "Hello there, little explorer." He sounded like a middle-aged man, and Feather instantly detected friendliness in his voice.

"Hello, sir," said Feather cheerfully. "Are you working on the Sphinx?"

"Why yes," said the man. "There has been a lot of wind this year, and sand has collected and hidden roughly seven inches all around the Sphinx. We are cleaning it up and adding an invisible protective mesh layer to prevent any additional erosion and wear and tear from the wind scouring it with sand."

"*Wow*, that is incredible that you can actually create a hidden barrier to protect this monument. Will you eventually work on the entire structure?" she asked.

"That is the plan, little by little," said the man. "By the way, little one, please be extremely careful as we have unearthed quite a few scorpion nests, and many of them are right below the surface of the sand. They are not deadly," he reassured her, "but a sting from one to someone your size could be very painful and could possibly cause hallucinations."

Feather, who had never seen a scorpion before, asked him to explain more.

"Well," he said, "the ones we uncovered today are solid black and have eight legs like a spider. They have two large pincers in the front and a curled tail they hold upright in the air. Scorpions generally come in all sorts of colors, and a general safety rule is to be aware of the size of their pincers and their tail. The larger the pincers, the less dangerous they are. The larger the tail, the more deadly they can be. Big pincers mean less venom in the tail, and they need to protect themselves by fighting; little pincers mean more venom in the tail, and they protect themselves by stinging."

Wow, the animal kingdom is truly a diverse and remarkable place, Feather thought.

She assured the man she would be cautious, thanked him, and

told him a little bit about her quest. He listened attentively. When she had finished her tale, she said goodbye and turned to start making her way around the Sphinx. As she stepped away, the man said, "I love your hat, by the way! I notice it has had some wear and tear; you must have had it for a while."

Feather felt her face flush and knew that she must be turning three different shades of crimson. She smiled and gently lied to the man, "Thank you, yes, I have had it for quite some time now. It keeps the sun out of my face and helps me keep my cool on hotter days." Feather didn't want to tell the man that she'd only had it a day; it was much more than a hat; it was an outlet to channel her frustration. She was almost certain it would help her deal with sadness or fear in the future as well. Gnawing on her hat wasn't the best habit, but it served its purpose physically and mentally.

Feather walked carefully and slowly around the Sphinx, looking for any markings or etchings while trying to watch out for scorpions.

She realized that the Sphinx had a very long tail that wrapped around the entire backside. It didn't look like the tail of a feline but more like that of a dog.

She also noticed more vase-like drawings on different parts of the Sphinx. Were the ancient Egyptians big fans of cut flowers and vases, or did flowers in a vase have some significance pertaining to the afterlife? She would ask someone the next time she thought about it.

As she continued to look for a sign or a message on anything, she slowly realized that there were no clues. None! *OMG,* she thought, *why does this have to be so difficult? Why did I have to even follow this crazy riddle? It just doesn't make sense. Why, why, why?* She looked up at the blue sky, shook her head from side to side, and emitted a low-pitched growl that transitioned into a howl that she usually reserved for full moons or UPS and Fedex drivers.

She sat down again near the Sphinx's left front paw, and held her own head low.

"Patience, patience, you will get there," she repeated to herself, but sadly her words of encouragement just didn't feel authentic at this point. She needed more. She needed her friends; she needed hope.

She lifted up her head and said directly to the Sphinx, "Give me a sign!"

Nothing! Just silence.

Humph, she pouted, *it must be sleeping.*

She rose to her feet to walk back to the hotel when she noticed

a large rectangular tablet that she had somehow overlooked before. It was full of pictures and lots of hieroglyphics. It had to be a message of some sort. "Thank you," she said, blowing a kiss to the Sphinx. *But now I just need to know what they mean so I can interpret the symbols.* She slipped the rim of her hat into her mouth and found herself chewing it again.

Am I missing clues? she wondered. *If only I could read these hieroglyphics.*

She sat back and closed her eyes. *If I was supposed to have been able to read the hieroglyphics in the riddle from Anubis, he would have told me that,* she mused. *And so far, everything that I have found or seen pertaining to the riddle has been very clear. The Land of the Cobra. When the city disappears.*

She opened her eyes, took one final look at the Great Sphinx, and headed back toward the hotel. Inside, she went to ask Mohammed about the stone plate with the hieroglyphics and vase drawings, but he had already gone home for the night. Her curiosity would have to wait until tomorrow.

Although her limbs dragged somewhat with disappointment on the way to her room, since she was not yet in the Land of the Cobra, she would not give up until she had found all the clues.

CHAPTER EIGHT

KING TUT AND THE VALLEY OF THE KINGS

Who knows if a nose really knows best?—Rehtaef The Canis

Feather glided into the small Luxor Airport after a one-hour flight from Cairo, having navigated the mini turbulence in stride. "I realize, to many people, I must seem like a bit of a world traveler," she casually mentioned to the lady seated next to her. The woman didn't speak any English but politely smiled and nodded.

Less than an hour after arrival, Feather gingerly boarded the *Mermaid of the Nile,* a luxury cruise ship that held seventy-five people comfortably. She squealed with delight when she found her bed decorated with adorable animals made out of towels, toiletries, and napkins.

"Drop your bags off in your cabin, and then meet me on the dock at the ship entrance in ten minutes," said Zara, the cruise tour guide. "You'll have the next couple of days to enjoy your room and sail up the Nile, but for now, we need to stay on schedule to take our bus out to the Valley of the Kings."

Feather packed two bottles of water and raced down the ship stairs to meet the guide. The town of Luxor was beautiful with streets lined with date trees; a warm, temperate climate; and the bustle of a busy, larger town. She hoped she would have time to explore it this evening after the Valley of the Kings and before the cruise started down the Nile.

"Hello again," said Zara. "So today, you will be visiting the Valley of the Kings, the most famous burial area in the entire world. Ancient pharaohs sought welcome in the afterlife and brought their most important earthly belongings with them but were worried that grave robbers and future pharaohs would thwart their plans. So they devised an ingenious way to prevent this from happening—they built tombs in the solid limestone mountainous region of Luxor in a remote, desolate area. These tombs had only one entrance that was completely camouflaged with internal traps and secret passages to hide the king and his most precious items. It is believed that the individuals who buried the kings and knew of the location were blindfolded on the way to the Valley of the Kings so as not to know the exact location. Then they were paid handsomely to relocate to another part of Egypt where they would live the remainder of their years."

I can't imagine, thought Feather, *being willing to completely shift your life for the secrets of a pharaoh.* And then as Feather continued to think about it, it didn't seem all that strange. She would have followed her mom anywhere. "I understand," she said. And she truly did.

"Today, you will have the opportunity to visit a total of three different tombs," said Zara. "Since today is a weekday, chances are we shouldn't have to wait in any lines. Now is the time to start planning which three tombs you would like to visit."

Feather asked, "Is there any chance that Doctor Hawass will be here working on one of the tombs?"

Zara smiled. "That would be absolutely amazing! In all honesty, I have wanted to meet him my entire life," she said, "but he probably isn't even in the country. I'm afraid the odds of meeting him are about as great as discovering a new hidden passage here in one of the tombs."

Oh well, Feather thought, *I can always dream!*

Feather listened carefully to the different descriptions of the tombs she could visit and decided she would visit two of them: Seti I—known as tomb KV17, the most elaborately decorated of all the tombs—and KV62, the tomb of Tutankhamun. She would spend the majority of her time in King Tut's tomb, where she hoped to find her next clue.

"One quick caution," mentioned Zara, "there have been some electrical surges the last couple of days, and power has been going off unexpectedly. If that should happen when you are in a tomb, a low emission black light will come on, so it won't be completely dark. In that instance, it is recommended that you just sit down, and someone will come down with a high-powered lamp to help you return to the surface. There is no need to be concerned or panicked," she said.

Feather smiled. Because of her amazing canine abilities, she would see fine in low light if she had to.

As she followed the signs toward KV17 — King's Valley 17, also known as Seti the First's tomb—she was amazed at how arid and barren the land looked. *What a great place to hide a king*, she thought. There was literally nothing here, no vegetation, no trees or plants. There were just small signs annotated with a KV designation and dusty orangish-brown rocks.

She followed the rocky path for a few minutes into a darker passage leading directly into Seti the First's tomb.

As she descended the stairs into the mouth of the tomb, she passed by worn hieroglyphics on the walls with very weathered pictures, some in muted, subtle colors.

This looks interesting enough, she thought. Twenty-five more feet, and there was a gentle turn.

Wow! Feather marveled at the most beautiful, vibrantly painted pictures and scenes in full color, sharp in detail, and laid out in progressive storytelling about the intricacies of ancient Egyptian life.

As she continued down another 400 feet or so, colorful relief paintings and shapely, carved ancient pictures covered all eleven chambers, including the actual burial room.

The lights flickered and then shut off for about five seconds, and then came back on and stayed on. The ceiling above was arched and glistened with ancient astrological scenes. Feather found it easy to read the story of the afterlife and how the pharaoh communed with his people and the gods in the pictures. She could barely contain her awe at all the beauty.

Time froze as she read, and before long, two hours had passed.

Feather made her way back to the guard and asked which way to King Tut. He pointed a long weathered finger and said, "Hurry. It will only be open for about thirty minutes or so due to some electricity challenges."

Mouse whiskers, she fumed. She put the rim of her hat in her mouth and chomped down, biting into her frustration. *I am here to track down clues for the riddle, and the most important tomb I need to see will be closing in thirty minutes. This is total bull horns!*

She found the tomb of King Tut unguarded and carefully climbed down the steep stairs.

When she entered the burial room, she stepped back in shock—his head and feet were sticking out from a covered piece of tan cloth. She had no idea she'd actually see King Tutankhamun's mummy! He was completely black, very compact, and surprisingly small. Feather took in a deep breath and just stared. She reached to put her hat in her mouth but then stopped. She wasn't scared or nervous or even repulsed—just curious. This young man had died more than 3000 years ago, and yet here was his body completely contained. Amazing!

Suddenly, with a loud pop, the lights just went out. Then a low hum began before a subtle violet black light cast an eerie, yet relaxed pallor over the body of the ancient king and the rest of the room.

She took another breath and gently settled down onto her belly and waited. Surely within a few minutes she would see the light of a large flashlight coming down the passageway. Any minute now, she was sure. She could almost hear footsteps coming down the hall. She waitcd and waited but nothing. *Hmmm,* she wondered, *maybe there were more people needing help in the other tombs. Wait a minute,* she thought, *there wasn't a guard at the entrance when I entered. Maybe they don't realize I'm down here!*

She grabbed her hat, and just as she was about to start some serious chewing, a faint blue-and-green glow radiated from a crack on the far side of the wall floor behind the mummy of King Tut. She needed to squeeze under the container that held the mummy of King Tut without touching it. So she dropped super low to the ground on all fours and used her Stealth *Kippy* Crawl, which she had learned from her older sister years ago.

She went right up to the crack in the lower wall where the light was seeping through. *What is that?* Trying her hardest to see the source of the greenish glow, she pressed her little black nose into the crack to smell the source. The dry plaster was surprisingly soft. She pressed further, with more force this time, against what felt like a flap or a springboard door. She pushed and pushed, but it wouldn't budge, so she pulled her little nose back, and—*OUCH*. Her nose caught on something sharp, and she yelped in pain. She'd been punctured! She could smell her own blood. As she wrestled to get her nose free, she felt the wall open, and she slid down past the flap. She closed her eyes to prevent dust and debris falling into them. After sliding a couple of feet, Feather landed on a floor. It wasn't a hard landing, more of a comfortable slide, but her nose was sore, her eyes were still closed, and she could now smell stale air.

Feather opened her eyes but didn't move. A bright greenish-blue creature sat three inches from her nose. It was about the size of a small mouse and had two pincers facing toward her, eight legs, and… oh no, a curved tail held up in the air with a single drop of venom at its tip. Feather was looking eye to eye with a scorpion!

Feather stopped breathing and started whimpering. The man at the Sphinx hadn't mentioned this color of scorpion, so she looked

carefully at the tail, and even though it probably wasn't very big, it looked huge to Feather.

"Oh, thank the gods!" said the scorpion. "Seriously, I thought I was a goner."

"You? I thought I was the goner," Feather said.

"I saw this massive furry black thing coming at me, so I struck and ran."

"You struck me with your tail?"

"I was afraid you were going to eat me. I hate the black lights; I can't help but glow when they come on. I didn't mean to hurt you, I promise. I was just scared." And just like that, the scorpion scurried away.

Happy to realize that she was still alive but irritated by the pain and tingling in her nose, Feather looked around and found herself gazing at a statue of a woman's face. There was just enough light coming from the small tunnel to make out her face and her neck. The young woman was adorned in gold and jewels and looked quite familiar. She reminded Feather of the face in gold in King Tutankhamun's mask.

"Well, I am in King Tut's tomb after all. Maybe this was his mother or his sister. She is absolutely beautiful," Feather said out loud.

"Why thank you. I haven't been paid a compliment in thousands of years," said the statue.

Feather's jaw dropped open. "You can talk? How is that possible? Who are you?"

"Well," said the statue, "I only have a couple of seconds to speak to you before you—it is possible I am speaking because—and my name is Nef—" She abruptly stopped before fully completing any of Feather's questions. "Well, my name isn't important. What is important is why are you wasting your time here when you need to complete your quest? You are supposed to be in Lower Egypt figuring out the clues that Anubis carefully left for you."

"But that is why I am here, Nef. Can I call you Nef?" asked Feather. "I am looking for the remainder of the clues!"

"No, no, no," said Nef, "there are no clues here. Get to Lower Egypt. There isn't much time. Now you need to climb back up into the tomb, and you only have a couple of seconds until—" And then the statue froze again.

Feather obeyed, climbed up the little slope that had dropped her into this room, and carefully crawled under King Tut's box.

The hidden door closed quietly, and no light emitted under it like before.

Suddenly dizzy, Feather looked around, lost her balance, and fell over on her side, all paws splayed at different angles.

CHAPTER NINE

THE NILE AND THE NUBIAN VILLAGE

Someone's fear may be someone else's joy.—Bob the Pharaoh

Feather shielded her eyes from the bright light as she opened them slowly to a gentle rocking and a whispered voice.

"Hello, welcome back, little dog. I am Ahmed, the captain of this ship." The voice belonged to a man in a long beige robe and a simple, yet nautical hat. "It looks like my littlest passenger decided to have a wrestling match with a scorpion, is that right?"

"Hello," said Feather, lifting herself onto all fours while still getting her bearings. "I remember talking to the scorpion and then to the statue of Nef, but I don't remember much more. I am pretty sure I was in King Tut's tomb."

"Yes, you sure were," said Captain Ahmed, "They found you crumpled up on the floor in front of King Tut's mummy. At first, they thought you must have gotten frightened in the dark by the mummy, but then they saw the puncture on your nose and figured it must have been a scorpion."

The captain thought for a moment and then asked, "Did you say you talked to the scorpion and the statue of Nef?"

"Yes," said Feather, "I frightened the scorpion, and it spoke to me for a minute, and then the statue of the beautiful lady started speaking with me about my quest."

"Oh, I see," said Captain Ahmed. Smiling kindly, he said, "I have a feeling you have experienced the side effects of the scorpion sting. Hallucinations are common. Maybe you had been speaking about Queens Nefertiti or Nefertari earlier in the day?"

"I don't know those names," stated Feather, "but Nef was very beautiful and very direct about me returning to my quest."

Feather frowned. The captain clearly didn't believe her, yet she knew in her gut that she had spoken to the lady Nef and the scorpion as well. *Well, it is my quest, not his,* she thought.

"I am glad that you are back from the land of sleep and here to enjoy the last of our cruise on the Nile. We visit the Nubian village later today and then sail tonight for our surprise in Abu Simbel tomorrow. We are arriving on a very, very special holiday."

"But wait, this is an eight-day cruise," said Feather, "Abu Simbel is our final destination, which doesn't happen for a week."

"We are wrapping up the end of our trip," said the captain. "You have been asleep for the past five days."

"Five days?" exclaimed Feather. "How is that possible?"

"Scorpion venom is more powerful than you could imagine, especially for someone your size. I am just glad that you are better now and get to relax before our village visit later.

"We have about four hours until we land outside the Nubian village, so feel free to go to the upper deck for a wonderful buffet or take a swim. It might give you some relaxation and reinvigoration before our village visit."

Feather thanked the captain for his kindness. Then she looked out her floor-to-ceiling window at the expanse of water and land in the distance. The Nile was massive, with blue glittering water and beautiful palm tree reflections in every direction.

She was soon distracted by a low rumbling gurgling sound and looked down at her skinny belly. "I'm sorry you have been neglected," she said. "Let's get you taken care of." She headed toward the sundeck.

When Feather stepped onto the upper deck, her senses went into maximum overload. Her nose gifted her with the smell of carved wild turkey, drippings of tender roast beef, and foreign meats that seemed to be calling her name. Her fur collected the warmth of the sun radiating off the Nile and the gentle breeze blowing softly over every inch of her body. Her eyes delighted her with thousands of lush green tropical trees; tall, fertile sand-covered hills; and beige-and-red

brick buildings of every shape and size. *You're not in Cairo anymore, Feather.*

Feather grabbed a plate of the deliciously carved meats and a few vegetables for good measure. Thirty seconds later, the meat was gone but the vegetables, not so much—those she would generously save for someone else. She casually sauntered over to the deck-top pool.

Feather wasn't the biggest fan of taking a bath, but she loved stretching out on her back and dipping her toes in the water. So she elongated her little body and let the sun kiss her belly as her two back paws were gently teased by the water that rocked to the rhythm of the boat. Right before falling asleep, she thought that this was a lifestyle she could get really used to. Feather enjoyed the feeling, and then she was sound asleep.

Then the ship's bell rang four times followed by Captain Ahmed speaking.

"Docking in fifteen minutes. Please meet at the main deck for the Nubian village."

"Marhaba and hello again," said Zara, "we are going to walk a kilometer to the Nubian village to see how a different group of Egyptian people live their daily lives. We will see how they make clay pottery, how they create reed baskets, and maybe, if we are lucky, we can even get a henna tattoo."

Zara instructed them to wait outside by the side of the ship. "That is where our tour will start, and today I might be able to introduce you to the famous pharaoh, Ramses II."

"But wait a minute," said Feather, "wasn't he the massive statue in the Grand Egyptian Museum?"

"Why yes, he was," said Zara, "but this Ramses is unique to here." She winked at Feather.

Feather told Zara that she would meet them there, and then she ran like the wind. She preferred running to walking. The road was simple to find, and she arrived at the lush oasis four minutes later.

The oasis was an enormous tranquil body of water surrounded by palm-lined shores, multicolored tropical flowers, and lush vines. Water shot up from a quiet fountain, and a small sign read, *Respect and cherish your oasis, and Ramses will bless you with his protection.*

Feather looked over her shoulder but didn't see anyone. *Well, when opportunity knocks,* she thought and climbed between the lower and the middle metal cable surrounding the oasis. She was sure she would hear the rest of the passengers as they gathered closer, but for now, she would indulge her new favorite pastime.

She let her back paws dangle just a few inches into the water, looked up at the sun, sprawled out on her back, and closed her eyes. Within seconds, Feather was sound asleep.

Feather startled awake to the sound of loud hollering.

She rotated her head to see where the commotion was coming from, but the sun blinded her.

She shielded her eyes from the sun and saw Nubian villagers running toward her from the left. *How strange. I wonder what happened?* She looked to her right and saw Zara and the other passengers running from the opposite direction toward the Nubians.

What is going on? Is there an emergency in the village? Did someone get hurt? Still unable to see very well, Feather took a step backward and now had all four paws in the water. The voices and the screams grew louder, more intense. Feather's heart raced at the unknown. She watched the action play out as if in slow motion. Was there a natural disaster?

"Tim saw who, Tim saw who!" the villagers shouted repeatedly. *Are they talking about someone named Tim?* she wondered. *And who exactly did he see?* Now she could hear the distinct cries from Zara and the other passengers yelling, "Ramses!" Yes, they were yelling Ramses.

She couldn't figure out why everybody was shouting for Tim and Ramses.

Before she could make sense of it, Feather was distracted by the sounds of separating water directly behind her. Instinctively, Feather turned and flipped in the air 180 degrees to face the oasis and landed about four feet up on the shore away from the water.

There, ten feet from her, an enormous, incredibly ugly greenish-gray log sped through the water, about to crash into the shore.

Feather bolted up and away from the oasis at the sound of a loud hissing noise. Within three long leaps, she flew between the middle and lower wire cables and kept running without looking back.

She finally stopped about twenty feet past the oasis cables.

When Feather turned and looked back at the log, she was greeted with approximately sixty of the sharpest yellow teeth that she had ever seen. This most certainly wasn't your typical log.

The "log" barreled through the water and onto the shore mere inches from where Feather had just been sunbathing and wrestled to push its massive body under the lower cable toward Feather. Feather watched, horrified as this moving log started bending the metal poles that were holding the cable. The log wasn't stopping, and its intended target was Feather.

Right at that moment, a group of Nubians flew past her and started smacking the ground with their hands while hissing at the log. Some of them threw small stones at the shore. The log stopped trying to get past the cable, and just as quickly as it had emerged from the water, it flipped and reentered the oasis, completely disappearing.

Feather was shivering uncontrollably from head to tail. She barely spoke. "Let me guess… 'Tim saw who' must mean 'alligator'?"

"Not quite," said a very tall Nubian man. "Timsawho means 'deadly water lizard'. And you, little Anpu, just met Ramses, our sixty-year-old, nineteen-foot crocodile. He is normally our village's good luck charm. But, I daresay, he wasn't necessarily yours today."

Feather nodded. *That was an understatement,* she thought.

Feather didn't walk into the Nubian village after that; she was carried, swaddled like a small baby as Zara sang her Nubian children's songs to help calm her down.

Finally, as her heartbeat returned to normal, Feather sat down inside one of the Nubian homes. "Everything we could possibly need is given to us from the Nile," said the mother of the house. "When we need water, we take the clay from its shore and make pots to carry it into our home. When we need to eat, we fish in its depths, and it provides us plentiful nourishing food for our bellies. When we need to carry goods and supplies, we take its reeds and create lightweight, yet strong baskets that allow us to share with others. The Nile is a member of our family; it watches us, protects us, provides for us. It is our child, our brother, our father," said the mother, gesturing and smiling.

They had a simpler, more ritualistic life than Feather had expected. Considering what she had just experienced, it sounded incredibly peaceful and relaxing.

Feather, now feeling like herself again, smiled at all the little children who kept running up to touch her on the head while saying, "Welcome, welcome, my little Anpu." Feather had always loved children, and their gentle touch and hugs made her feel special and calm.

The mother of the Nubian home delicately framed Feather's face with her hands. "Right here," she said, gently touching both cheeks, "I will place a very unique and special henna tattoo. We shall honor your great fortune in our village today. It will not be permanent, but it will last for a couple of weeks." Feather accepted with delight.

While the mother gave Feather the henna tattoo, Feather showed off her own special tattoo below on her belly.

"What is it, what does it mean?" asked the Nubian children.

"It is a very special tattoo given to me by my mom. She fitted me with a tracking device so that if I were ever lost, she would always be able to find me."

"That is protection, that is love," said one child, touching Feather's tattoo. "But what is the significance of the symbol?"

"It is a little heart, and it means that wherever I go, and whatever I do, my mom will always love me and be proud of me."

The children all agreed that it was a wonderful tattoo to have but commented that it was a very unusual design for a heart. "I never would have known it was a heart unless you had told us," said one of the children. "Our hearts look different and have—"

"Your tattoo is finished," interrupted the mother. Feather looked at her new henna tattoos in the mirror. They were beautiful, intricate hieroglyphics coupled with Nubian characters.

"What do the symbols mean?" Feather asked.

"They mean 'Anpu who tricked Sobek, the crocodile god.'"

"I love it, thank you," said Feather.

Later that night as Feather waited for the boat to rock her fast asleep, she thought about her dangerous adventures over the past few days: first her encounter with the scorpion and now the crocodile. She promised herself that tomorrow she would do everything within her power to stay out of harm's way. After all, tomorrow was her final day to uncover the clue she needed on her quest here in Lower Egypt.

CHAPTER TEN

ABU SIMBEL

The sweetest success starts with the toughest failures.
—Huntram IV

The warm breeze gently parted the fur down Feather's back as she sat on the small triangular point on the bow of the ship. Today was her last opportunity to uncover the secrets of the riddle. What if she traveled all this way to Lower Egypt and never uncovered the clues to understand her mother's message? "Rabbit ears," she said, "I will have great success today!"

A little later on the bus to Abu Simbel, Feather promised herself she would not get distracted. Her singular goal today was the final clue. *The place of dreams will illuminate your heart.* Would Abu Simbel be the place of dreams?

When they arrived at Abu Simbel, Feather was blown away by the sheer enormity of the twin temples. *Was everything always this grand, this big, this amazing in Egypt?* Outside the entrance of the main temple stood four massive statues of Ramses II, beckoning one to come into the shade inside.

Feather made her way into the first of the two temples; this one was called the temple of Nefertari, the wife of Ramses II. Inside the temple loomed sky-high pillars covered in intricate hieroglyphics carved right into the massive mountain. Feather diligently walked up and down every single row—all thirty-seven of them. Alas, nothing stood out. *Come on,* she thought. *Where is my clue about the dreams? Where are you?*

She left the temple and headed to the larger of the two. This was the temple of Ramses himself. Four massive statues outside all faced east.

Feather repeated her previous pattern, walking down each and every aisle in the temple looking for anything that stood out. Anything that was different. Anything that would give her insight into the clue about the place of dreams, but alas there was nothing. Absolutely nothing. She tore into her hat with her upper canines with fervor, shredding a brand new hole in it.

At last, she dropped her head in defeat and made her way toward the temple exit. If music accompanied our moods, Feather's would have been a dramatic, defeating piece.

As Feather left the temple, a rising breeze pushed gently on her, forcing her to lose her balance and exit a little quicker than she had planned. Suddenly a gust of air pulled her hat off her head, and it flew about fifteen feet in front of her. She ran after the hat but couldn't quite catch it. She lunged at it and missed it again, landing face-first in the dirt.

She looked up, caught in a shadow and felt even more defeated. Two dusty boots stood in front of her, and she saw a familiar silhouette but was unable to see the face because of the sun. The figure wore a hat just like hers. He bent down and handed back her hat.

"Thank you," said Feather. "Dr. Hawass? Is it you?"

"I'm sorry, I'm not him," said the man. "I'm Jony, and you are quite welcome."

Without any warning, Feather's body started shaking uncontrollably, and she broke down into sobbing and tears.

"Hey, hey, hey, what's the matter, little one?" asked Jony.

Talking through tears, Feather said, "I am so sorry. I am having a horrible day and honestly was hoping you just might have been someone else."

"Tell me about it," said Jony. "I am an archeological student studying ancient Egyptian studies in Cairo. How can I help?"

Jony sat down next to Feather, put his hand supportively on her back, and just listened. The words poured out of Feather like an uncontrollable river. Feather explained the dream, her travels from the United States, and finding all of the clues but the last one.

Feather then read Jony the riddle.

"Follow your heart, and it will guide you. Search in the Land of the Cobra, and when the city disappears, the place of dreams will illuminate your heart. Peace and understanding will then be forever yours.

"I followed all the clues," said Feather, "and then got stuck at the Sphinx. But I figured I was okay because the riddle said I needed to be in Lower Egypt, the Land of the Cobra. So I headed south. First to Luxor and King Tut's tomb, and now I am here at my final destination in the most southern part of Egypt, and nothing. No final answer to the riddle. Nothing." Feather's voice cracked, and she half spoke and half cried, "Now I will have to leave never having understood the riddle or what my mom needed me to know."

"Feather," said Jony, "I have some good news and some bad news for you."

Feather looked at him with tear-drenched eyes. "If I am being completely honest, I don't think I can handle any more bad news."

"Well then," said Jony, "let's start with the good news, okay? I know where you need to go to understand the last line of your riddle."

"You do?" Feather asked, jumping excitedly to her feet. "Where is it exactly?" she asked, looking around. "Which temple is it in?"

"Sadly, that is the bad news. It isn't here. You need to return to the Sphinx in Giza. The answer to the last clue of your riddle is at the front of the Sphinx."

"But that doesn't make sense," said Feather. "The riddle specifically said that I needed to be in the Land of the Cobra. And Lower Egypt is the Land of the Cobra, right?"

"Yes, you are 100 percent correct," said Jony, "Lower Egypt is indeed the Land of the Cobra. But here, right now, you are not in the Land of the Cobra! You are not in Lower Egypt right now. Giza and Cairo are in Lower Egypt."

"Wait, that doesn't make any sense. I am confused," said Feather. "I am here in the most southern part of Egypt, which is Lower Egypt."

"It can be a little bit confusing. Let me draw this out for you," said Jony, who grabbed a pen and paper from his backpack.

"Upper and Lower Egypt are not based on north or south locations," he said, drawing the Nile River. "Upper and Lower Egypt are based on the direction that the Nile River flows.

"So the Nile River enters Egypt from the country of Sudan, which is south of Egypt. It flows from the southern part of Egypt here in the south to the north where it enters the Mediterranean Sea. That part is called Lower Egypt because the river flows down through it.

"Does that make sense?" Jony asked. "So basically, Upper Egypt is in the south, and Lower Egypt is in the north."

Feather was speechless. What felt like a minute went by.

She looked at Jony and could only say, "So I need to go back to the Sphinx?"

"Yes," said Jony. "There is a tablet at the front of the Sphinx that tells a story about a place of dreams. I am sure that it is the final clue to your riddle. Just ask one of the guards or someone near there, and they will show it to you and explain its significance."

Feather leaped into Jony's lap, almost knocking him over, and said, "Thank you, thank you, a thousand times, thank you!"

"You are welcome, little one. I wish you great success on the rest of your quest. I know you will discover the message your mom has for you."

"How do you know?" asked Feather.

Jony smiled. "I have faith in you!"

He waved to Feather and walked away.

Feather was still in shock. It was horrifying that she had been traveling the wrong way all this time, and yet the wonderful news was that she knew where to go from here. She raced through the temples until she found Zara. "I need to get back to the ship to pack everything and fly out tonight back to Cairo and then to Giza."

"Feather," said Zara, "you are not going to want to miss the surprise parade this afternoon. It is a very important and unusual holiday that people travel great distances to watch. Besides, there won't be any flights out this evening, only the one we prebooked for tomorrow morning."

"I really want to come," said Feather, "but I need to head back to the ship to make arrangements to go directly to the Sphinx tomorrow morning. Once I am done at the ship, I may come back out," she promised.

"Okay," said Zara, "but keep an eye out for the festivities as you head back to the boat; you might see some parts of it on your way there."

Feather hugged Zara and thanked her again for supporting her after the crocodile incident. Zara smiled and said, "Any time, little Anpu, any time."

Feather dashed off and jumped into a taxi out front of the temples. "To the *Mermaid of the Nile,* please," she said.

"There are many crowds for the Festival of the Anpu," the driver said, "so we are being rerouted through town at the moment. Just know that traffic will definitely be slower than normal."

"The Festival of the Anpu? They have a festival for that?" Feather asked.

"Why yes," said the man. "September 10th is our appreciation and adoration of the Anpu day. People come from all over the world for this holiday and for the very unique camel parade."

"Wow," said Feather. "What an incredible country that takes the time to celebrate Anpus like me!"

The driver smiled, making a gesture toward Feather's face tattoo. "Yes, you are indeed a very good-looking little Anpu."

As Feather pondered the idea of a festival of new friends, she became aware of the crowds and the redirection of traffic. There were people walking outside who were moving faster than the taxi.

"I am sorry, my friend, but it looks like traffic is not going to let us get there very fast. It may be quicker for you to jump out and just walk back toward the pier."

Feather thanked the man, jumped out of the taxi, and made her way through the crowd. She walked parallel to where the parade would be happening.

Suddenly Feather heard, "There you are, Anpu. We have been waiting on you. We didn't think you were going to make it! Let's go." And with that, Feather was picked up and placed on someone's shoulders.

Feather had no idea what was going on, but she was headed in the direction of the pier, and, at this height, she moved quite quickly through the crowd.

"We are almost there," said the man carrying Feather. "We have everything laid out and ready for your outfit."

"Wait," said Feather, "I think you made a mistake. I am on my way to the pier."

"There will be plenty of time for whatever you need to do after the parade, little Anpu," said the man. "By the way, your henna tattoo is perfect. 'Little Anpu tricks the crocodile god.' Very clever! If it wasn't for the tattoo, I never would have seen you down there on the ground, and wouldn't have realized that you had arrived."

"But I am confused," said Feather. "Aren't there other Anpus that you want besides me?"

"There are always lots of Anpu candidates," said the man, "but you are perfect. You *are* our Anpu, and that is why we picked you. Out of the way, out of the way!" shouted the man. "The Anpu needs to be prepped."

"Okay, we are here. Here is the plan," said the man. "We have only ten minutes. Mariam here will be doing your makeup, Omara will fit you for your outfit, and Jasmin will perfect your headdress. Any questions?"

Feeling completely confused but honored that they chose her out of all the different Anpus, the new friends of Egypt, Feather decided to be flexible. She would head back to the ship after the festival, and she could nap on the plane in the morning if she needed to.

Feather was seated in an open upstairs courtyard, and within seconds, three individuals were hovering around her like bees. She felt rather important.

First her hat was removed and tucked into her backpack, and then she was fitted with a golden-and-black robe, followed by a headdress and a golden collar. Mariam, the woman doing her makeup, said, "Unlike the henna, this makeup will only last until you shower." They tweaked this and adjusted that, and then finally, she was done.

A few minutes later, Feather was escorted under cover of full cloak into the square below. Seven massive camels stood waiting. Feather was amazed at the unique beasts whose bodies seemed out of proportion. It instantly reminded her of the Sphinx in Giza.

The man who had originally carried her through the crowd yelled a word to an enormous camel, and suddenly the massive animal dropped its legs below itself and sat on the ground.

The man lifted Feather onto the camel and placed her in a special saddle that allowed her to stand on either two or four legs without losing her balance.

"You mean I am going to ride him?" she asked in amazement.

"Yes, little Anpu, you will be on the first of seven special camels led through the crowded street for eight blocks. You are our most special Anpu, and everyone will want to greet you and ask for your blessing.

"As soon as you hear the cannon fire," said the man, "I want you to throw down your cloak, and I will give your camel a gentle pat on his behind, and you will start the parade. The only thing you have to do is wave at the crowd and maybe give them a howl every once in a while," said the man.

"A howl?"

"Yes, please, if you don't mind."

Feather made sure she was secure in her saddle. When she heard the cannon fire, she threw off her cape, and the crowd around her went wild.

Her camel started moving, and all she could hear were the cheers and shouts. Feather had never been cheered this way before. She felt like a movie star.

The crowd started chanting in unison, "ANPU, ANPU, ANPU." Feather adjusted her two back paws solidly and stood up, raised her front two paws to the sky, and gave the howl of her lifetime. The crowd cheered and hollered as though they just couldn't get enough of Feather, this little Anpu. She couldn't stop smiling!

All of a sudden she heard, "Feather, Feather, is that you?" She looked down toward her side, and there was Zara, smiling up at her as she walked beside the camel.

"Oh my goodness," Zara said, "you completely fooled me. I thought you really had to go back to the boat. But you were secretly our little Anpu. I can't believe you were the main attraction this entire time. You are the most wonderful Anpu ever. Truly the best living Anubis I have ever seen."

"Anubis?" asked Feather. "I don't understand. Why would you call me Anubis? Isn't this a celebration for new friends? The celebration of the Anpu?"

Zara looked confused for a minute. "But Feather, Anpu doesn't mean 'new friends.' Anpu is the ancient Egyptian word for Anubis."

"Anpu means Anubis?" said Feather. "You mean all this time I have been called..." and then she stopped, not quite able to fully process what she had just heard.

Zara reached into her purse and pulled out a mirror. She stretched up and handed it to Feather. The face staring back at Feather in the mirror was no longer her own but that of Anubis. She was a smaller identical image of the Anubis of her dreams. Feather handed her back the mirror, and the camel continued to make its way through the crowd.

"I will meet you at the end of the parade," shouted Zara. "Thanks again for keeping your identity a surprise. You really, really tricked me."

Feather was numb, as if she had stepped into the path of a car with its bright lights coming directly at her. Once again, Feather attempted to process all those people who had called her Anpu. In reality, they had actually been calling her little Anubis! *Goat hairs!*

Well, she thought, *if I am called it, so shall I be it.* And Feather continued waving back at everyone, and she howled—oh, did she howl. She gave the crowd exactly what they wanted. She gave them Anubis, and she had never felt more excited or proud.

At the end of the parade, Feather gave her garments back to the man and thanked him for choosing her.

"Thank *you,* little Anpu," said the man. "We were so worried when we got the call earlier that your plane was delayed and not coming in today. Thank goodness you made it. You were the best Anubis we have ever had."

Feather decided that the kindest and most honorable thing she could do was to let him believe that she had been the original one chosen for the parade.

"Thank you," she said.

He handed her a necklace with two distinct pendants on it. One was a golden feather, and the other was a golden vase similar to the one she had seen in multiple locations around Egypt.

Zara hugged Feather and then gathered the other passengers. Feather had never needed to come to southern Egypt on her quest. But look at all the adventures, all the opportunities, and all the people she would have missed.

Feather touched her new necklace and contemplated its significance as she hurried back to the ship.

CHAPTER ELEVEN

THE MAN IN THE HAT

Once you find your path, anything is possible.
—The Book of Gwendolyn the Wise

After an uneventful flight, Feather's plane touched down in Cairo. She raced through the airport and past the baggage claim to the awaiting taxis. Her hat, now in tatters, barely stayed on her head, but the single ear sticking through an "accidentally" chewed hole kept it from falling off her head.

"To the Sphinx, please," she said to the taxi driver.

"Oh no," said the driver, "I am so sorry, but they are finishing up some preventative repairs this week. No one is allowed to enter."

"No! Please tell me it isn't so. It can't be!" she said.

"Little traveler, I am sorry, it is true. I can take you there and show you if you would like?"

"Please," said Feather, "I have to get inside! It's where I need to be. This can't be happening."

Feather's hat was back in her mouth, and she chewed on it with the vigor of a caterpillar chomping on fresh leaves.

When they arrived at the front of the Sphinx, Feather thanked the driver and jumped out of the taxi. The driver was correct—it was completely blocked off by a large chain-link fence.

She approached a guard standing in front of a locked entrance.

"Excuse me, excuse me, please," she said. "I have been on an incredibly important journey. I just flew in from Abu Simbel, and there is something at the Sphinx that I really need to see."

"Sorry," said the guard, "but that just won't be possible. We are under strict orders to keep all tourists out this week."

"But, sir, please, I don't think you realize how very, very important this is to me. Please, sir," begged Feather.

"With all due respect, there is absolutely no way that you will be going in to see the Sphinx today!" the guard said pointedly.

While Feather was thinking of anything that would help this guard to understand her plight, a man covered in a brown protective face mask walked over and asked, "Is everything okay, Kamil?"

"Oh, forgive me, I am so sorry for the disturbance, sir, but this little…tourist is insisting she needs to see something at the Sphinx. I explained to her that it was forbidden, but she is an American, and she continues to insist."

"It's okay, Kamil. I will vouch for her."

Feather recognized the man's voice as the worker she had spoken to on her last visit to the Sphinx.

"Thank you, seriously, thank you. You are a lifesaver!" Feather said.

The man smiled. "So tell me, little one, how is that quest of yours coming?"

Feather explained her grand mistake of confusing Upper and Lower Egypt. She told him about falling down in Abu Simbel and being in total distress thinking she would have to leave Egypt without ever understanding her mother's message.

The man nodded then asked, "So what led you back to the Sphinx?"

She explained how an archaeological student named Jony told her that this was the likely location of the final part of her riddle.

The man's eyes crinkled as though in a smile behind his protective mask.

"Well, I would say that something, or someone, really wants you to have a successful quest. You see, Jony is my student and was the other man helping me last week when you were here."

"What an amazing coincidence. No wonder he knew that I needed to come back here," said Feather.

"It is a very, very common misunderstanding about Upper and Lower Egypt," said the man. "Many of my students just assume that rivers don't flow up in a northerly fashion, but when the topography is higher in the south, the river flows down to the north. Sorry, did that make sense?"

"Yeah," Feather said, smiling, "I definitely understand it now. Are you a teacher?" she asked.

"In many ways, I am," he said, removing his face mask and grabbing a hat from his bag.

"I am an Egyptologist, and my name is Dr. Zahi Hawass."

Feather's throat was suddenly dry, and all that came out when she tried to speak was a low guttural gurgle. She grabbed her water from her pack, took a swig, and just stared and stared.

Finally she broke her silence. "Dr. Hawass, it is such an honor to meet you. My name is Feather Ramey, and you are the reason I am on my quest. I had no idea before that I was speaking to you. I am a little starstruck, in all honesty."

He laughed. "How kind of you. These protective face masks

really do allow one to be anonymous. Please, sit down, Feather, and tell me of your adventures on your quest. Would you share some tea with me? It is decaffeinated."

"Thank you, yes," said Feather, and she sat down next to Dr. Hawass and told him everything that had happened since she first had her dream and saw him on YouTube.

"So our Anubis actually reached out to you and gave you the riddle? I have heard of Anubis showing up in people's dreams many times but never giving them a riddle or putting them on the quest to communicate information from a loved one."

Dr. Hawass hesitated. "However, if I am being honest, it does sound like something that Anubis would do. He has been known to come up with very unique ways to connect our two worlds." He laughed gently. "May I look at that riddle of yours?"

Feather handed him the now very worn paper that Egress had originally written the riddle on.

Follow your heart, and it will guide you. Search in the Land of the Cobra, and when the city disappears, the place of dreams will illuminate your heart. Peace and understanding will then be forever yours.

"Okay, so you are here in the Land of the Cobra, in Lower Egypt." He smiled slyly at Feather. "I am guessing you saw the unique corner of the pyramid where the city disappears and that brought you here to the Sphinx, the place of dreams?"

Feather nodded. "But Dr. Hawass, why is this considered the place of dreams?"

"Thousands of years ago, Thutmose IV was king only of this part of Egypt. He fell asleep during a very hot day and had a dream. In the dream, the sun god came to him and told him that where he lay was an enormous monument, a Sphinx that had been buried under years of sand. He was told that if he were to uncover the Sphinx and restore it to its previous glory, he would be made king of both Upper and Lower Egypt. This would have been a tremendous feat.

"So the king listened to the sun god, unburied the Sphinx, and became king of both regions of Egypt. Where you and I sit at this very moment is the place of dreams."

"Right here? Right now?" Feather looked down in amazement.

"Yes, indeed! The Sphinx has always been magical," said Dr. Hawass. "It connects our world to the world of our unconscious. It makes sense to me now why this would be the final part of your quest. There are those out there who believe that the Sphinx connects this world with the afterlife."

Feather was momentarily at a loss for words.

"Thank you, Dr. Hawass, that makes sense, but I wonder what the place of dreams has to do with understanding my quest?"

"I'm really not sure, Feather, just that the riddle says the 'place of dreams will illuminate your heart.'"

"Maybe I just need to take a nap right here on the place of dreams, and I will have another dream that will clarify everything," Feather said.

"That sounds like a good guess," said Dr. Hawass. "And it is almost noon. Actually, 11:58 is the time the king had his dream. It is the point of connection where ancient Egyptians believed the sun god was closest to the Earth, when magical connections are possible."

"Really?" said Feather. "I always get sleepy and take naps around that time as well!"

"I love your necklace, by the way," said Dr. Hawass. "It is wonderful. How clever that you wear the two most important symbols of Anubis—the symbol for the feather and the symbol for the heart."

"The symbol for the heart?" asked Feather.

"Yes," said Dr. Hawass, showing Feather the sides of the amulet.

"This is where the blood goes in, and here where it comes out."

"But I have seen this symbol all over Egypt, I thought it was a vase." said Feather.

"Why yes, I suppose it does look like a vase," said Dr. Hawass. "But the heart is one of ancient Egypt's most important symbols for both this life and the afterlife."

Dr. Hawass looked down at the riddle again and said, "And the place of dreams will illuminate your heart. It will illuminate your heart." He repeated the saying once again, and then he became quiet for a moment. "Feather, I am wondering…" He paused. "On the south side of the Sphinx, there is a barely noticeable partial carving, and we have wondered for years if it might have been a carving of a heart. Did you happen to notice it when you were last here?"

"I might have walked by it," said Feather, "but I honestly didn't notice it."

"Maybe now that you have the clues, that is where you should go?"

"Absolutely," said Feather, and she got up and started walking south to the side of the Sphinx.

She turned around. "Dr. Hawass, are you coming?"

"Thank you, I would love to," he said, "but this is your adventure, your quest. It was you who Anubis contacted."

Feather glanced at this man, clearly wise beyond his years, and gave him a respectful acknowledgement with her head.

Feather headed to the south side of the Sphinx, searching for what looked like half of the heart on her necklace.

She thought she saw it, but honestly it was not very pronounced, and it had been so weathered it was barely noticeable at all.

This couldn't be it. She walked closer. *Or could it?*

As she walked toward the etching, a most peculiar thing happened. A subtle pink glow emerged.

She stepped back, and the glow went away. She walked closer, and there it was again.

The glow wasn't coming from the Sphinx. It radiated on the carving of the Sphinx but only as a reflection.

She looked down and then she saw that the pink glow was coming from…her heart tattoo.

She touched it. It didn't feel any different, but it was emitting light. A radiant pink light.

She walked closer to the Sphinx, and her heart tattoo got brighter and brighter.

She was now a couple feet away from the Sphinx. As she continued closer to it, almost within touching distance, her necklace with the symbols from Anubis lifted off her little chest and was pulled toward the Sphinx.

Feather took a final step and placed her paw on the Sphinx. Her heart tattoo grew brighter, and a dagger-like streak of pink light erupted from the faint etching that had been on the Sphinx before.

She held her paw firmly on the Sphinx, and the streak of light started moving, creating a path on the Sphinx, tracing where the heart had been. It was literally cutting a heart out of pink light.

Feather didn't move her paw, and the light continued to move completely around her paw, around her body, etching a perfectly formed Egyptian heart.

Feather stepped back. The inside rock of this new carving suddenly vanished, and all that remained was an enormous heart lit in the most vibrant pink light.

Feather stepped forward and carefully caressed the light. She timidly put her tiny paw into the light, and it partially disappeared.

She jerked it back instinctively, but her paw was fine. All she felt as she touched the light was a peaceful warmth.

Feather looked way over toward Dr. Hawass, who was near the front of the Sphinx. He smiled and winked at her.

Feather closed her eyes and took a step forward directly into the radiant pink heart of the Sphinx…and within seconds, she disappeared inside.

CHAPTER TWELVE

THE DOG AND THE HUMAN

Goodbyes are temporary, love is eternal.–Yrtsed Rose

As Feather slowly opened her eyes, all she saw was pitch-black nothingness. *Should I walk forward here in the dark?* she wondered. *Should I wait? Do I turn around? What exactly do I do?* For the briefest second, she began to doubt her decision to have entered the heart, and then, as her eyes adjusted, a distant electrical blue light flashed about fifty feet in front of her.

Feather stared in the direction of the lightning-like flash. A dark blue bridge was materializing directly out of the air as if created from the electrical storm.

As it became easier to make out the details of the bridge, Feather noticed something on it—a figure. Yes, there was definitely a figure standing there. It appeared to be an animal of some sort and not very large. The figure moved very slowly in her direction. Feather didn't blink. She refused to allow her eyes to wander away from this creature. She just watched, subtly aware of the tension in her muscles as she prepared for the unknown.

The animallike figure was proportional to her own size. However, there was something odd and distinct about its movements. It walked with an assertive confidence, almost as if it were marching across the bridge.

It continued to move closer and closer toward Feather, and then about twenty feet from her, it abruptly stopped and sat down with all four paws tucked below itself.

It was a dog, yes, it was definitely a dog, and she instinctively sensed that it was male. But what surprised her is that it felt familiar.

She couldn't quite understand it, but it looked, felt, and even smelled like her.

It reminded Feather of staring into one of those carnival mirrors that took reality and distorted it into a variation of the truth. Was she somehow seeing herself walking toward her?

Feather stared firmly into this creature's eyes, this mirrored version, without showing an ounce of emotion. This creature, this dog, stared right back at her, mimicking Feather's facial expressions completely.

Still completely on guard and ready for anything, she watched this spitting image of herself as it lifted back up onto all four paws and slowly continued walking toward her.

Fifteen feet, twelve feet, now it was only ten feet from her. Feather attempted to step backward, away from this approaching version of herself, and yet her paws wouldn't move. Her muscles would not respond, as if they were no longer hers to control.

This mirror image of Feather was now only eight feet away from her, and then just like before, it abruptly stopped.

The sky filled with electrical activity, and a single lightning bolt struck the dog directly. As the bolt hit the canine in front of her, all of its fur and physical attributes, almost all semblance of the dog itself, disappeared. All that remained were the dog's underlying muscles.

And then something even more incredible happened.

The dog lifted its front paw muscles overhead and pressed into the lightning bolt. Its body began to vibrate, to shake, and it grew extremely quickly—its back legs transformed into adult human legs, its two front legs and paws formed into human arms and hands. Within seconds, Feather was looking at a large human adult with the head of a dog. Feather was now eight feet away and looking directly into the eyes of the ancient Egyptian god Anubis.

For what felt like an eternity, Anubis looked at Feather, examining every inch of her, and then he shifted gently into a smile.

"Well, well, well, welcome, my little Hafida," said Anubis. "You finally made it here."

Feather, in awe of what had transpired, said, "Yes, I am here. Hafida?"

"It wouldn't make sense for us both to be called Anpu, or Anubis, now that we both are together, would it?" he said. "How would anyone ever be able to tell us apart?" Once again, he smiled, this time playfully.

"I am here to congratulate you, Feather. You finally figured out my clues, put together my riddle, and now here you are. I was a little worried at times as you headed down south, but your determination and perseverance allowed you to be here today. I am very, very proud of you!"

"Thank you, it has been quite the adventure." Feather blushed. "It wasn't easy, but I am glad to be here now." Then, suddenly aware of what was occurring, she said, "I can't believe I am talking to you, the god Anubis."

Anubis smiled. "Feather, what exactly do you think a god is supposed to do?"

Feather paused, reflecting on this unexpected question.

"Well, I am still learning about different beliefs, but I suppose we look to a god to guide us and give us directions when we are lost or feeling alone," said Feather.

"Good," said Anubis. "What else?"

"Obviously a god helps us and gives us comfort when we are frustrated and overwhelmed."

"Excellent," said Anubis. "Anything else?"

"Well, I would say most importantly, a god loves us unconditionally and lets us know that no matter how alone we might feel, they are always there right by our side."

"I couldn't have said it better myself," admitted Anubis. "These are indeed the most important traits of a god. Feather, I need to tell you a secret," said Anubis. He paused. "I am not a god."

Feather almost completely inverted her head, thinking, *Did I just hear what I thought I heard?* She didn't say a word.

Anubis continued, "I am simply a loyal companion who shows people the path to get to where they need to go. I comfort those who feel hopeless and troubled along the journey, and when they feel worried, afraid, or alone, I give them hope and love."

"But aren't those the qualities of a god?" asked Feather.

"Yes, they are," said Anubis. "Feather, why have you traveled thousands of miles on a journey to understand a message from your mom?"

"Because I would go anywhere or do anything for her."

"Would you protect her if she asked you?"

"In a second."

"Even if it meant putting yourself in danger?"

"Without hesitation."

"Did you love her for her entire life?"

Feather took a moment. "No," said Feather, "I will love her for *MY* entire life. I will love her forever."

"Feather," said Anubis, "one of the greatest secrets in human history is not that I am a god, but that I am a dog. My actions, loyalty, and unconditional love represent the closest thing possible to being in the presence of a god here on earth.

"In fact, I even left the human race a few reminders," said Anubis. "For example, in English, if you write the word 'god' backward, it spells 'dog'. There is nothing that is more godlike than loving someone unconditionally.

"You, Feather, represent more than 35 millennia of canines whose job is to remind humans what it is like to know and be in the presence of unconditional love."

Feather's heart swelled with pride.

Anubis smiled again.

"However," said Anubis, "you are not here to uncover our secrets for the human race. You are here to understand the afterlife and how that pertains to your mother. You came all this way to understand the message that she has for you."

"Yes," said Feather, "please tell me her message for me."

"Oh, Feather, I am sorry. While I do indeed know her message, I am afraid that it isn't mine to give you."

"Oh no," Feather said. "Please tell me that there isn't another part to my quest."

"No, not quite, little one," Anubis said, stepping to the side.

Feather looked at Anubis, waiting for insight, and that is when she saw it. On the bridge, now moving in her direction, walked another figure.

The figure came closer and closer, but before Feather could even make out the face or had heard the voice, she knew who it was.

Feather recognized the walk; she recognized the scent, and she instantly felt her body being drawn toward this figure. The pull Feather felt on her heart was undeniable.

The figure in front of her was Mom. Her mom!

Feather, unable to contain her emotions, ran past Anubis, jumped onto the bridge, and, within seconds, leapt into the air and landed in the arms of her mother.

Tears upon tears of happiness flowed from Feather. "Mom, Mom, I have missed you," is all she was able to say. Feather had never felt so completely overwhelmed with love and joy. In fact, Feather felt so flooded with happiness, she forgot to breathe and started hyperventilating.

"Shhhhhh, shhhhhhh, I am here, little one, I am here. Your mom is here with you." Mom patted and rocked her gently.

Feather gasped twice, inhaled deeply, and caught her breath. She rubbed her head into her mother's neck and face, licking her with kisses.

Even clasped tightly in Mom's loving arms, Feather just couldn't get close enough to her. She pressed her bowed head into her Mom's warm grasp with no other thought then to never let Mom leave her side again.

"Hello, Littlest Angel. I sure have missed holding you," said Mom.

"You came back for me," said Feather.

"I have been waiting for you. I need your help," Mom said.

"What is it, Mom? What do you need? I would do anything to help you and for us to be together."

"I know, my little Feather," said Mom, "and that is why I wanted to see you so that you could understand. I need your help so I can continue on my journey to where I next need to go."

"Of course, Mom, of course. Anything! Did you want me to guide you, walk side by side with you, and protect you along the way? Is that why you sent for me? You know I would go anywhere to be with you. I love you more than anything," said Feather.

"Yes, Littlest Angel, I know you do," said Mom. "I know you'd follow me. I know that. But this isn't the time for your journey, little one. It isn't your time yet."

"But Mom," Feather said, "I can't help you if I can't be with you."

"Well, actually you can," said Mom.

"But I won't leave you. I don't want to say goodbye. I want to be with you."

"Feather, even though you haven't been able to physically see me like before, I have been there the entire time with you. I sent the message to you through Anubis because I have heard and felt the tremendous sadness that you have been carrying with you. There have been so many tears, so much pain, so much frustration. Feather, there was no way I could continue on my journey without giving you a sign, without helping you to understand that I am all right, that I will continue to be okay."

"So even after our time together here on Earth, you are still watching over me?" asked Feather.

"Yes," said Mom. "However, I, too, need to know that you are going to be okay, that you will be able to find peace."

"But I have missed you so much. I sometimes wonder if I even can continue on. It feels like my entire life has died when I think about you not being here," Feather sobbed.

"Feather, I need you to listen very carefully to what I am about to say. Will you do that for me?"

Feather meekly agreed.

"Feather, one of the beautiful surprises of the afterlife is that all your pain, suffering, and even the memories of difficult challenges dissipate completely. This leaves us with only the joy, happiness, and love that we have experienced in life. Do you think that knowing this can help you to ease your pain?"

"I had no idea," admitted Feather. "I think so, Mom."

"There is not a word or words appropriate enough to express the amount of love, joy, and pride that you have given me. I have learned and been given so much by being your mother. I have acquired knowledge and obtained qualities that I would have never known without you in my life."

"But, Mom, how will I go on?" asked Feather. "How will I continue without you here?"

"Feather, I will always be here with you. I just will be watching

you from a different place, a different plane. I will be there with you to celebrate your triumphs and victories and smile with you when you are happy and feel loved. I will be watching when you are sad, and I will send you a message of comfort to remind you that I am right nearby and that you are loved. I will always be there with you.

"It is because of you that I truly know what it is to love unconditionally. You have opened a world to me that I would never have known without you. Feather, please know that when you see an angel, a mermaid, or especially a feather, that I am nearby.

"Never forget that you are compassionate, sensitive, and loving, and stronger than you can even imagine. Do you know that I love you with all my heart and soul?"

Feather nodded. "I do."

"Then, Feather, will you allow me to go, knowing that you will be okay, that you will continue on and be brave for me?"

"Will it make you happy?" asked Feather.

"More than anything in the world," said Mom.

"Then of course, Mom, yes," said Feather. "I would do anything to make you happy."

"Remember that I will always be a thought or a whisper away. Enjoy life for me, my incredible and wonderful daughter, and strive to keep the balance."

"I will," said Feather, "I will. I will always, for as long as I live."

"Then it is time for me to continue on my journey," Mom said.

Her eyes flooding with tears, Feather gave her mother the tightest hug she had ever given.

"I love you, Feather."

"I love you too, Mom."

And with that, Feather's mom turned and walked across the bridge. But with each step she took, the bridge changed from dark blue to a bright mist that dispersed and disappeared.

Mom turned around and waved, and Feather mouthed the word 'ITALY', eyes full of tears.

"I love you too, my Littlest Angel."

Her mom took another step and disappeared.

Feather had completely forgotten about Anubis until she heard, "Hafida, your quest is complete, and you have received the message from your mom."

"I have," said Feather quietly. "She needed my help…" She paused for what felt like an eternity. " …To say goodbye."

Anubis nodded reverently and vanished. And just as quickly as she had entered, Feather was once again staring at the weathered partial drawing of an ancient Egyptian heart on the outside of the Sphinx.

CHAPTER THIRTEEN
THE DOG IN THE HAT

Love never leaves us, it just changes form.—The Wisdom of Angels.

And then there was light. And also sweltering heat. And Feather, her nose as dry as the surrounding sand, needed to move out of the intense rays of the afternoon sun. She had to come back into this plane, this reality, not only physically but mentally. But how do you go back to your reality, your world, when everything you want and everything you love is in a different one?

Somehow, she willed her body to move. She lifted her feet and started walking away from the barely perceptible carving of a heart. She made it about ten steps, and then she spun around and raced back to the carving on the Sphinx. She thrust her little front paw and placed it solidly on the heart. And…nothing.

Of course, why would anything happen? Why would she be transported into a different plane, a better plane, one where her mom was?

So she stepped away from the Sphinx again and walked toward Dr. Hawass. He sat at the place of dreams, looking into the distance and sipping his tea. When she approached him, he looked at her without showing any sign of emotion.

Feather sat down next to him and allowed her weight to gradually shift next to his side so that she was gently touching him. She grabbed her hat, placed it in her mouth, and stopped. She was aware of its presence, but she didn't chew it, she just…tasted it. It was salty and slightly dusty and smoky, and it tasted of leather. She pulled it from her mouth, took it off her head, and just stared at the hat. During her many days of frustration and unknowns, this hat had given her comfort and the ability to channel her concerns.

Now, it didn't feel right to bite it. Feather had no desire, no need whatsoever to chew on her hat. And for the first time since Mom had died, she didn't feel sadness. Surprisingly, she also didn't feel any frustration either. What then did she feel? She felt love—oh, so much love—and…was that hope? It had been a long time, but she recognized the buoyant rise of hope.

Dr. Hawass cleared his throat and picked up and reread the riddle Egress had written. "So is it true? Will 'peace and understanding now be forever yours'?"

"I'm not 100 percent sure, but I think so," said Feather. "I definitely will need some time to process everything that has occurred and just let it all settle in."

"That makes a lot of sense. Feather, I don't know if this will give you some perspective or not, but someone wise once explained life

to me this way." Dr. Hawass put his hands in front of himself about shoulder width apart. "This space between my hands represents our life." He gestured with his left hand. "This represents the beginning of our life." He gestured with his right hand. "This represents the end of our life." Then he moved his right hand all the way over so it was almost touching his left hand. "And this right here represents when we die here in this world."

Feather followed his hands closely.

"Death here on Earth isn't the end but just another beginning. The process of dying allows us to slide from one world into the next. You will never be separated from your mom; she just slid into another part of her life before it is your time for you to join her. You will be with her again; you just have some unfinished plans that you need to complete on this plane first."

"Thank you, I appreciate that, and I understand," said Feather. "But I don't like the idea that I have to wait, that I can't just join her now."

"Well, let me tell you about a huge advantage that you have as a dog," said Dr. Hawass. "Your time passes differently than ours. Because you love so intensely and are so incredibly devoted to your mom, your time has been sped up and magnified. Every day you spend on Earth takes us a week to pass the same amount of time. Every year you spend takes us seven human years to catch up as well. This difference in time allows you to participate in unconditional love extremely quickly. Then when we separate, just a few years go by, and you get to experience all that love with us again. Does that make sense?" he asked.

Feather nodded, loving the idea that she would get to see her mom again in a different passing of time.

"The most important thing you can do is spend every day here making the best of it and honoring your mom in the process."

Feather felt a heavy weight release from her chest. It was now okay for her to continue, okay for her to say goodbye to Egypt. So she got up, put on her hat, and thanked Dr. Hawass. "I guess it is time for me to be going," she said.

"What's next?" asked Dr. Hawass.

"Well, it's time for me to go back home and share my experiences and adventures with my family and friends," she said.

"Will you be coming back to Egypt?" asked Dr. Hawass.

"Absolutely," said Feather. "It feels like there will always be a part of me here in Cairo. I can't quite explain it, but Egypt feels like another home now."

Dr. Hawass smiled and nodded gently.

"Thank you for everything, Dr. Hawass. You will never know just how much you have helped me. Thank you." She gave him a hug.

Feather turned and started walking in the direction of the exit. She reached down, felt her heart tattoo, and smiled. Feather didn't know what would come next for her, but she realized that wherever she would go, Mom would always be there, keeping an eye on her until they could be together again. Feather's chest warmed at this thought.

Feather stepped outside the entrance to the Sphinx, walked for a minute, and then heard someone calling her name. She turned around and Dr. Hawass was walking briskly toward her.

"Feather, now that you have completed your quest and have a new level of peace and understanding, your chewed-up hat probably won't serve you anymore."

Feather touched its wrinkled surface. "Even though it is in tatters, I am sure I will continue to travel and try to understand more about life and the afterlife."

"My thoughts exactly," he said.

And with that, Dr. Hawass removed Feather's hat, took off his own, and placed it on her head.

"Feather, I want you to have my hat going forward." Dr. Hawass' hat was considerably larger than Feather's hat had been, and it slid down and completely covered her eyes.

Dr. Hawass chuckled and slid it back up her forehead and tightened the strings so that it fit her.

"Here is the secret—take it home and wash it a few times, and it will shrink right up until it fits you perfectly."

Peeking out from under her wonderful new gift, Feather said, "I will never ever forget you."

"Nor I you. Bye, little Anpu."

"Goodbye, Doctor."

And with that, Feather turned to the sun and walked toward her destiny.

EPILOGUE

Only at the end can we truly understand our beginning.
—Pharaoh Phreaking

Feather kept her paws carefully centered on the small steps leading up the pyramid. She never thought she would find herself here in Mexico at Chichen Itza, and yet she cautiously put one paw after the other and climbed to the closed off passageway leading to the center of the pyramid. Unlike Egypt, here it was moist and tropical, and even though Feather didn't sweat, everything was misty and slippery. Everything smelled of moist tropical rain and jungle leaves, even the pyramid itself. Feather finally made her way to the top, and as she entered the narrow inner chamber and made her way down the long passageway, she saw a light up ahead that appeared to be a lantern. She walked closer and found a dark figure standing near the end of the corridor holding a torch.

"Come, Hafida, let me see your face in person again." She instantly recognized the voice. "I have been observing you these past months since we met, and I am pleased that you have been living peacefully and with purpose. But now it is I who comes to you asking for your help. I need a living relative of mine on Earth to assist a family that has lost all hope."

"Anubis, I am so glad to see you! You have a living relative here on Earth?" Feather asked in surprise.

"I do." Anubis smiled.

"A close… associate of mine, Mictlan—you can call him Mick—will reach out to you and tell you more in the future. Would you be willing to help me, Feather, my little Hafida?"

"Of course, Anubis," said Feather. "I can never thank you enough for helping Mom and me to have our last chance to be physically together. I would be happy to speak with your friend and to help to find your relative here. Do they have any idea that they are related to you? And how do I even start to try and locate them?"

Anubis grinned. "No, they don't know they are related to me yet, but they will soon. How you locate them is easy; in fact, you already have. I gave you the clue before, Hafida. The answer is in my name for..."

Feather was jolted awake by the clock radio. She had been dreaming again. She rolled over, curled between Egress and Daddy Chris. She was about to wake up Egress and tell her about her dream when she heard the song "Family Secret" by Ramona and the Black Pearls come through the radio. She found herself paying attention to the catchy rhythm and lyrics.

He said I'd know the secret.
I just had to wait.
Would I have to wait forever
or just deliberate?
The thing that you are missing
is the thing you always knew.
The mirror reveals the secret.
Is the clue now coming through?

I leave this final message
as I start to make my way.
The truth is we're connected
in more than time and space.

No, it couldn't be, thought Feather. *Or could it?* She jumped out of bed, raced over to the computer, and typed in the word "Hafida."

Feather looked at the translation on the screen in disbelief. It read…*"granddaughter!"*

ACKNOWLEDGMENTS

Losing a parent is never an easy process and, if we are fortunate, never a solo task. If we are blessed, we have those souls along our path who not only support and listen to us but also help to lighten our pain and suffering along the way. These individuals remind us of the remarkable moments of laughter, adventure, and especially love that we shared.

I want to thank each and every one of you who has made this journey easier for me with your patience and support. I appreciate your stories, your anecdotes, and your revelations of the surprising bits of my mother's history. I thank those of you who have been kind enough to let me emote, tear up, relive memories, and finally move into a place of peace.

I owe more than I can possibly express to more good people than I can count. However, there are a few specific people and a certain dog who believes she is a person who have had the most profound influence on my mother, me, and this book:

SARA WILLIA: From the moment I first accidentally stumbled upon your artwork, I knew that you had to be the one to illustrate this story. You surpassed my expectations in creating this deep tapestry of emotion out of my words and thoughts. Without your inspiring eyes along the way, this book would not be the rich, jeweled project that it became. The fact that you and Mom were connected and yet never met or spoke still stuns me to this day. And your final drawing, which holds the most profound secret of this entire story, will always be ours to share. Thank you, Sara!

JORDAN ROSENFELD: Without the work of this amazing author and wordsmith, this book would never have come to fruition. You are an editing genius, and your critical eye, which always steered me in the right direction, proved invaluable and allowed me to take this book to another level. I am forever grateful for that day that I heard you speak and hoped you would join me on my journey. Thank you for giving my book life!

DR. HAWASS AND THE TEAM AT ARCHAEOLOGICAL PATHS: Thank you, Dr. Hawass, for opening up the splendor, joys, and mysteries of Egypt. I so appreciate the company that connected us and the one-on-one time that you spent with my mother and me. I will never forget your generosity, and I hope that I have honored you in this book. Mom and I had the adventure of our lifetime experiencing the heartbeat of your country; I sincerely hope others are as fortunate as we were.

CHERYL LEHMAN AND PEGGY WATKINS: Thank you for the months of listening to every chapter of my early drafts, critiquing the book, and inspiring me to step aside from doubts while honoring my mother in the process. Your kindness and patience are greatly appreciated.

GWEN BAKER: Thank you to the most brilliant human and friend I know. I'm grateful for our weekly stimulating conversations and discussions about the complexity of navigating this world. Thank you also for giving me my first godson, Jack, who will continue to grace the world with his kindness and wisdom, just as his parents do.

DEBRA EARLE: Thank you for being my life changer! You are the person who not only inspired me in my career but also forever rerouted my life path and views on what is and isn't possible. Everyone should be so blessed to have someone like you in their life.

NICOLE SCHNEIDER: Thank you for allowing me to step into your world and life's work and sharing your ideas, talent, and passion with me. I'm grateful for your incredible support during these past few years, especially in validating the nuances of being a flawed human. Please know without a doubt how much I appreciate you and your brilliant insights.

DARIN PASTOR: You know I love you, brother, and will forever cherish our friendship and the amazing lessons you gave me. Thank you for always supporting me. I will always be thankful for your ingenious mind.

PACO ILLANES: Thank you for your unwavering support all these years, always taking the time to check in and consistently being a voice of reason.

DR. MISHA SHAH: I never thought I would meet another medical professional with the incredible level of empathy, professionalism, and compassion my mother exhibited. Then she told me about you, someone she deeply admired. Your heart is enormous, your skill is incredible, and your kindness and understanding are second to none.

LINDA, BOB, AND CALI REID: Thank you for making Feather and me a part of your family. I appreciate your generosity of time, food, and sharing holidays with us, and thank you for giving Feather her new little sister.

DAN MCCOSHUM: Thank you for being such an incredible and loving part of Mom's life. Thank you for always having her back.

MIKE YOUNG: Thank you for being a hidden hero, delivering years of good advice. Also, for letting Mom and me reap the benefits of your time, patience, and talent.

LINDA AND JOSEPH MARCHITTO AND RICK SCRUGGS: Thank you so much for your kindness and generosity, continued support, and delicious food. I am so grateful that our paths crossed.

MARIO CRUZ: I appreciate you, brother, and am so glad we have kept in touch all these years since our time in the military. I look forward to more international adventures together.

EMILY PASSIC, SUMMER MEYER, ERIN AKER, AND JEN HERSMAN: To some of my favorite people of all time. Who would have thought that a chance meeting on a massage table years ago would lead to a lifetime of friendship? I appreciate your videos, your insightful knowledge on health practices, and for consistently making me laugh.

INGRID PIRES: Thank you for being such a wonderful and kind soul.

I so appreciate you making Mom's transition process easier. You have no idea how much your knowledge and kindness led to peace and relief.

DR. DAVID PALCHAK: Thank you for the effort, hope, and patience that you gave both Mom and me. I appreciate you and your incredible staff.

DAVE CONGALTON: Thank you for being such a kind friend to both Mom and me. I so appreciate you supporting her and her message through the foundation.

KATHERYN SICILIANI: Thank you for jumping to the rescue at a time when I just couldn't do it myself. Your graciousness, generosity, and incredible kindness are so appreciated.

LAURIE KING (FEATHER'S TRAINER): Thank you for molding Feather into the little lady that she is today, your kind friendship, and helping Feather to understand us humanfolk better.

YVETTE MASON: Thank you for using your boot, literally, to help me do something that I had put off for years. Your kindness, incredible knowledge, and professionalism made the impossible possible.

SUZY FARBMAN: Thank you for being such an advocate for those who have challenges. Your gift to draw emotion from words gives so many people a reason to be hopeful and teaches them to forgive. Thank you for the beautiful article you published about Mom. Much love and appreciation.

DENNIS WEIST: Thank you for being the first person to honor and support The Destry Ramey Feather Foundation, supporting animal rescue efforts worldwide. I will forever appreciate your generosity and kindness.

KATHRYN MICHELLE, ELIZABETA VIDOVIC, AND BELA VIDOVIC: Aside from being some of the kindest people Mom and I have ever known, I'm so grateful for the honor you have bestowed upon us.

Thank you for putting my mother front and center in your beautifully filmed movie *The Accursed*. During your memorial to her at the end of the film, I became overwhelmed with emotion. Thank you for giving me one more unforgettable memory of her and for placing her on the silver screen. THANK YOU!

ELLISA WULIGER: You are one of the most intelligent, considerate, and amazing people I know. Who would have thought that a random chance encounter would lead to a lifetime friendship. I appreciate you, your challenges, and the beautiful way you have adapted, modified, and blossomed into who you are. Thank you for speaking so highly of me and sharing my work with friends and family.

CONROY BROWNE AND CELINA HERRERO: Thank you for always supporting Mom and me, even without ever having met her in person. You guys truly are the cheerleaders in the background, and I appreciate your generosity and friendship.

DANIELLE BLAKE PRENTICE: Thank you for your years of love and support. I count myself blessed for the time we spent together in Ocean Beach.

ONEL SIRIA: You know what I mean when I say that you were her *favorite*, right?

THE JOHNSON AND TOOMAN FAMILIES. Thank you for your continued kindness and thoughtfulness. My mom always wanted a Greek family, and you gave her one and me as well. Feather and I adore your beautiful children, Elliana, Makayla, Sophia, Aria, and little William. You all are most appreciated.

BISH GODWIN: For my friend of so many years, thank you for being such a wonderful advocate for my mother and her books. I will always admire and appreciate you.

RUCHI KOVAL: Thank you for helping me to better understand the Jewish beliefs about the afterlife and for the article you published about me. תודה

JAMES GIBSON: Thank you for being an incredibly kind stranger and going out of your way to provide so much time, effort, and expertise.

JOHN SEVERIN: This thank you is for the years of kindness, and generosity that you showed toward Mom and myself. You treated her like gold, and I will never forget that or you.

LOWREE CHRIST: To my neighbor who inspires delight and happiness in Feather with your amazing cats.

PABLO ARMENDARIZ: I will always appreciate your initial motivation and optimism, thank you.

DAVID SEDARIS: I appreciate the way you encouraged my mother when she was writing her first book. Communicating with and motivating her was so incredibly kind. Where will our paths next cross? Tacoma, Sydney, the food court in Edmonds?

GALINA DWYER: I just wanted to thank you for being such a great advocate for me and for going out of your way. I appreciate your kindness and hugs.

TO MY FRIENDS IN MEXICO AND BAJA NORTE who have opened their hearts and culture to me these past twelve years, thank you for your kind heartfelt generosity. I want to especially thank:

- **JONY RAMIREZ:** Por tu amistad, amabilidad y el amor mostrado hacia mi madre y yo.

- **"AMÉRICA" AGUILERA Y CARLOS GONZALEZ:** Para los más maravillosos asistentes que una persona puede tener. Ustedes y sus familias han sido tan importantes para mi, me han bendecido todos estos años de trabajar juntos. Gracias.

- **BERNABE SOBERANIS:** Por ser el vecino más increíble, lleno de sabiduría y amabilidad.

Special shoutout and thanks to the following organizations for their support of me, my mother, and animals:

- **CALIFORNIA FRESH MARKET**: Thank you for the years of supporting my mother's work. I appreciate the special space you give to my mother's and my books, which are right up front at the checkout counter for everyone to see.

- **SPRINGDALE PET RANCH**: Thank you for keeping Feather's mind stimulated and occupied. Seeing her socialize and excited to play with all her canine friends makes my heart smile and gives my life balance. Thank you!

- **CHARLOTTE MEADE AND THE MEADE CANINE RESCUE**: Thank you for being such an amazing and supportive friend of Mom's. I so admire the incredible rescue work you do daily, in which you are literally giving old dogs new reasons to live and be happy.

- **SLO NIGHTWRITERS**: Thank you for your encouragement and kindness and for always supporting my mother's writing endeavors.

- **ERIC DANDURAND AND HARMONY GLASSWORKS**: Thank you for your incredible generosity and for giving me a beautiful reminder of Mom.

- **WOODS HUMANE SOCIETY**: Thank you for supporting my mother and her book, and congratulations on being the first recipient of the Destry Ramey Feather Foundation.

- **BEST FRIENDS ANIMAL SOCIETY**: Thank you for the work you do to ensure that the US is moving toward a no-kill animal rescue policy.

- **HOSPICE OF SLO**: Thank you for your incredible advice and support.

- **THE MONDAY MAHJONG LADIES**: Thank you for giving Mom years of thought-provoking enjoyment and for being kind, considerate, and supportive of her.

- **LISA NELSON AND PCPA:** Thank you for being such an amazing and kind friend to my mother and inviting her into the theater scene on the Central Coast. Please know how much I appreciate you.

- **TO ALL THE PEOPLE WHO HAVE RESCUED AN ANIMAL:** You are making a difference and changing the value of companion lives one animal at a time. Thank you, thank you, thank you!

And finally, but not least:

HUNTER, RAMONA, KIPPY, AND EGRESS: Thank you for the years of laughter and joy and your patience, forgiveness, and love as I started my journey into the lessons of responsible companion ownership. I will never forget you guys, and I look forward to when we are once again lying in a field of grass with a warm sweeping breeze, just content in each other's company.

FEATHER RAMEY: Thank you for your nonstop antics, your consistent cuddles, your boundless energy, and for making me laugh multiple times daily. Your mother really knew what she was doing by leaving you in my life. I love you, Monkey Rat!

www.ingramcontent.com/pod-product-compliance
Lightning Source LLC
Chambersburg PA
CBHW051112300726
48981CB00001B/102